"Stolen kisses are the sweetest," he murmured against her ear

She opened her eyes and stared dazedly at him, wondering if he'd felt anything special. "You call that passion?" she taunted, piqued that he was still in control of himself.

"No. I call this passion."

She saw the flare of desire in his eyes. Then his mouth claimed hers again, and his arms enfolded her, and his hands molded her body to his, and there was no holding back. No control. Not for either of them.

She heard him say, "Tomorrow," in a deep husky voice. There was a gentle disengagement, his hands steadying her before slipping away. Then he was gone.

EMMA DARCY nearly became an actress until her fiancé declared he preferred to attend the theater *with* her. She became a wife and mother. Later, she took up oil painting—unsuccessfully, she remarks. Then she tried architecture, designing the family home in New South Wales. Next came romance writing—"the hardest and most challenging of all the activities," she confesses.

Books by Emma Darcy

HARLEQUIN PRESENTS PLUS

1592—THE LAST GRAND PASSION
1632—THE SHINING OF LOVE

HARLEQUIN PRESENTS

1519—HEART OF THE OUTBACK
1536—AN IMPOSSIBLE DREAM
1555—THE UPSTAIRS LOVER
1570—NO RISKS, NO PRIZES
1579—A VERY STYLISH AFFAIR
1604—THE SHEIKH'S REVENGE
1659—A WEDDING TO REMEMBER

Don't miss any of our special offers. Write to us at the following address for information on our newest releases.

Harlequin Reader Service
U.S.: 3010 Walden Ave., P.O. Box 1325, Buffalo, NY 14269
Canadian: P.O. Box 609, Fort Erie, Ont. L2A 5X3

EMMA DARCY

In Need of a Wife

Harlequin Books

TORONTO • NEW YORK • LONDON
AMSTERDAM • PARIS • SYDNEY • HAMBURG
STOCKHOLM • ATHENS • TOKYO • MILAN
MADRID • WARSAW • BUDAPEST • AUCKLAND

ISBN 0-373-11679-9

IN NEED OF A WIFE

CHAPTER ONE

HE WAS a complete stranger. He had brought his three-year-old son to the same harbourside park Sasha had brought her nine-month-old daughter. In half an hour of desultory conversation across a sandpit where their children played together, all she had learned about him was his name, Nathan Parnell. He was also the sexiest man Sasha had ever met.

He made a pair of jeans and T-shirt look like indecent exposure. The casual but open affection with which he touched his son conjured up visions of the tactile pleasure he would give a woman. It brought goose-bumps to Sasha's skin.

And those riveting blue eyes. When she spoke they focused on her with concentrated interest as though she were the most important person in the world. Sasha found it difficult to tear her gaze away from him. Even when she forced her attention back to Bonnie, who was being entertained by his little boy, she was intensely aware of the man lounging on the grass on the other side of the sandpit.

'What I need . . .' he spoke in a musing tone, not so much to her as to the world at large, yet the deep baritone of his voice made her ears tingle with anticipation to hear what his needs were '. . . is a wife.'

Sasha's head jerked up, her dark eyes wide with shock. She quickly flicked the fall of her long black hair over her shoulder to cover up her reaction to the startling statement. She had been secretly envying Nathan Parnell's wife, and berating herself for having wasted so many years on Tyler Cullum while all the best men were taken. The whimsically appealing smile Nathan Parnell directed at her set her pulse racing.

'Tell me honestly,' he invited. 'Would you consider the position?'

Warning bells rang in Sasha's mind. Strangers who made odd propositions in a park were definitely to be avoided, no matter how sexy they were.

Her gaze quickly swept their vicinity. Most of the people who had been nearby earlier seemed to have wandered off. There was an old man sitting at one of the benches, reading the Saturday newspaper, a young couple under the trees closer to the water, two middle-aged women apparently watching the leisure craft sailing by on the harbour, all of them a fair distance from the sandpit and all of them strangers.

She probably looked like part of a family group, Mum and Dad and their two kids, and people in the city tended to steer clear of others' troubles. This was time to get out.

'I'd better be going,' she said, trying not to look too hasty as she began gathering the plastic blocks Bonnie had thrown around.

'You haven't answered the question,' Nathan Parnell reminded her, not exhibiting any discomfiture whatsoever. 'I need a wife, and to satisfy my curiosity I'd like to know whether you'd consider the position.'

'Definitely not.'

'Is there something wrong with me?' he asked.

With his attributes, he could probably have the choice of any woman in Sydney. He probably knew it, too. Sasha cast him a quelling look. 'I thought you were already married.'

'I was. Past tense.'

It gave her pause for thought. Maybe he was a widower in desperate need for someone to mother his little boy. Although why he'd pick on her, after the barest acquaintance, left a lot of questions up in the air. Was he impressed by her manner with Bonnie? Was that the only yardstick he had for a wife? Or did he find her attractive enough to fancy her in his bed, as well?

Curiosity prompted her to say, 'I don't want to raise a matter that might be painful to you, but what happened to your first wife?'

'She's gone. Hopefully to hell and perdition.'

It was certainly no salute to the woman he had married. Which gave Sasha every reason to be circumspect with this man. 'I'm sorry things didn't work out better for you,' she said, resuming her block-gathering. To keep him talking until she could make her getaway, she asked, 'How did she die?'

'She didn't. More's the pity,' he said with an edge of bitterness. 'Though the marriage wasn't a dead loss. I got Matt. Thank God he takes after me.'

'Then you're divorced,' Sasha deduced, wanting the situation spelled out.

'No other way out of the problem.'

Sasha knew how messy such problems were. She didn't have to divorce Tyler Cullum because they weren't married in the first place, but effecting a separation was just as traumatic as any divorce. She wondered how any mother could leave her child behind, as Nathan Parnell's wife apparently had. Then, with a spurt of her own bitterness, she supposed there were women, as well as men, who didn't want their lives loaded down with children.

Nathan Parnell took her silence for complicity and resumed his proposition. 'Consider the advantages. We could go back to the old way of doing things. Set up a marriage contract...'

'What makes you think I'm free to marry?' Sasha demanded, thinking he was assuming one hell of a lot in talking to her like this.

'No wedding-ring.'

'Many people think marriage isn't valid any more,' she argued, although it was Tyler's opinion, not hers.

The blue eyes blazed incredulity. 'You're still living with a guy who didn't bother to marry you when you had his child?'

'It does happen these days,' she flared at him, painfully aware of the mistakes she had made.

'Why isn't he with you?'

'Because...' It was none of his business, but somehow his eyes pinned her to a reply. 'Because I left him,' she finished defiantly. 'He wasn't good to me, and he wasn't good to Bonnie.'

'There you are. Same problem I had,' he said with satisfaction. 'We'd both be better served if we worked out a sensible contract. Set out what we're prepared to give to the marriage, and what we can expect from each other.'

'You're talking about a marriage of convenience.'

'Absolutely.'

'What about love?'

'Definitely out. It causes havoc and creates chaos. Turns sensible people into raving lunatics. The Greeks had it right. They called it Eros. The eighteen months of madness before passion cools and reality sets in.'

'Well, you might not think it's worth having, but I do,' Sasha said emphatically.

She grabbed her holdall and stuffed Bonnie's play blocks into it. Her dreams might have been tarnished by her experience with Tyler, but she was not about to give them up and become as cynical as Nathan Parnell.

'What did love do for you?' came the sardonic challenge. 'How long did it take you to find out your lover was a dead loss when it came to commitment and responsibility?'

She faced him with grim determination. 'It wasn't love. Not real, deep-down love. And I'm not going to settle for anything less next time around. If there is a next time. I'd rather manage on my own than compromise myself again.'

'How will you know this *real, deep-down love?*' he asked sceptically.

'I'll know.'

She wasn't at all sure of that but she stood up in disdain of any more of his arguments, then bent to lift Bonnie over her arm and brush the sand from her legs.

She was conscious of Nathan Parnell swinging himself into a sitting position but he didn't rise to his feet.

'It's pie-in-the-sky,' he stated mockingly.

'You can hardly say your attitude is normal,' she retorted.

'Normality is a fantasy. People aspire to it because they're so frightened of being themselves.'

'Well, now I'm free to be myself,' Sasha tossed at him.

'If you married me, you'd be even more free to be yourself.'

'Free?' She cocked a scornful eyebrow at him. 'Wouldn't I have to share your bed?'

'Minimally. Marriage isn't legal without consummation. Would once in a lifetime be asking too much of you?'

'Once! What kind of marriage is that?'

His eyes danced over her from head to toe, openly admiring the shining fall of her long black hair, the curves of her figure which were faithfully outlined by her T-shirt and jeans, the shapeliness of her long legs.

'Perhaps I could manage more if you really wanted me to,' he suggested, flashing her a smile that had the kick of a mule. His eyes held a definite glint of earthy wickedness as he added, 'You have lovely skin. Smooth and creamy. Must be like satin to touch.'

Sasha could feel the cream burning into fire-engine red as she remembered wanting to know how it would feel to be touched by him. Her gaze dropped to his hands, lightly resting on his knees, and she had a moment of lustful speculation that was totally unlike her.

Fortunately, Bonnie recalled her to her senses by squirming and crowing her eagerness to be returned to her playmate. Sasha hoisted her daughter up against her shoulder, holding her more securely, defensively.

'This is getting beyond the pale,' she said, her eyes flashing contempt for his concept of a convenient marriage. 'Where do you get such ideas from?'

He shrugged. 'They popped into my head.'

'So you ask the first woman you meet, or happen to be with, to be your...' Words failed her.

He grinned, totally unabashed. 'There is a certain zest to it, springing into the unknown. It could be a glorious adventure for both of us.'

'Or a trip to hell and perdition,' she reminded him with waspish intent, hoping he felt the sting in the tail. 'Don't forget that,' she added for good measure.

'Doesn't apply. No love involved.'

'Which is where I opt out. Thanks for the offer but it has no appeal to me.'

She leaned down to pick up her bag, telling herself she was crazy to have listened to him for so long, crazier still to feel tempted into listening some more. Sex-appeal was a trap. It faded fast once one got down to the nitty-gritty of making a relationship work. Tyler had conclusively proved to her that a relationship without love had no hope of bringing any real or lasting happiness.

'Can't I play with the baby any more?'

'I don't think the baby's mother wants to stay, Matt, and we have to respect other people's wishes.'

It was a gentle answer. Sasha saw an arm reach out and gather the little boy into a comforting closeness with his father, a loving touch that put an ache of yearning in Sasha's stomach. If Tyler had been like that with Bonnie... But he hadn't, and any last hope of him ever changing had died the night she saw him shaking their child as though she were nothing but a rag doll.

As she straightened, the bag firmly clutched in her hand, Sasha tried her best to project proud independence in turning away from the disturbing influence of Nathan Parnell's presence. But her heart caught at the mournful look in his small son's eyes.

She was well acquainted with the loneliness of being an only child. But Matt did have the love of his father. And Bonnie had her love. The last thing children needed was to be caught in the warfare of a relationship that wasn't based on love.

Reassured that she had done the right thing in leaving Tyler, and was doing the right thing in leaving Nathan Parnell, Sasha stiffened her spine and bestowed a warm smile on the little boy.

'Thank you for playing with Bonnie.'

'Can we play again another time?' he asked.

'I'm afraid not.' She saw the disappointment in his eyes. 'I'm sorry,' she added, then turned quickly and walked away, wondering how different their lives might have become if she could have given another answer.

In her abstraction she did not see the figure striding across the park on an intercepting course.

'Sasha!' he called.

She heard the strident anger in the voice. It arrested her mid-step. She turned towards the source, knowing already what she was about to see, knowing she was about to be involved in another confrontation, this one much more serious than the minor skirmish she had just played out with Nathan Parnell.

She knew the owner of the voice.

It belonged to Tyler Cullum.

CHAPTER TWO

SASHA watched Tyler approach. She had once thought him sexy, but now she saw him as nothing more than a slick sophisticate, consumed with self-interest. He was more smoothly handsome than Nathan Parnell, conscious of the latest fashions, stylishly lean, and affecting a temperamental moodiness that he considered artistic.

Why she suddenly thought of Nathan Parnell as warm and honest and earthy, she didn't know. Contrast, she supposed. Nathan Parnell was a bigger man, his strongly boned face marked with expressive character lines, his dark hair an unruly toss of waves that looked finger-combed, if combed at all. There was nothing artificial about him. He was comfortable with who and what he was and not frightened to lay that out to anyone else.

Sasha told herself she had nothing to be frightened of, either. She didn't have to please or appease Tyler any more. She was free to be herself and go her own way.

But all her fine resolutions didn't stop her stomach from twisting into a knot of apprehension as Tyler came to a halt in front of her. She stared defiantly into stormy grey eyes, deciding she had a definite preference for vivid blue.

'You could have told your parents which park you were going to,' Tyler sniped. 'This is the third one I've had to look through.'

'I don't understand what you're doing here, Tyler,' she said truthfully. 'You were glad to see us leave a week ago.'

He made a visible effort to control his irritation. 'Well, I was wrong, Sasha. Now that I've had time to think about it...'

'I've had time to think about it, too. I wasn't wrong, Tyler. For me, it's finished.'

'You're being unreasonable, Sasha. Just because I'm not as patient as you are with Bonnie...'

Her expressive dark eyes flashed contempt at his hypocritical excuse. It forced Tyler to a concession.

'All right. I'm sorry for blowing up, but she *was* driving me nuts.'

'She won't any more. If you'll excuse us...'

Before she could move, Tyler stepped forward and snatched her carrier bag out of her hold. 'You're not going anywhere until we've talked this out.'

Sasha fought to remain calm, disdaining any attempt to retrieve the bag. 'Talking won't make any difference to my decision, Tyler.'

She saw the struggle on his face. He found it difficult to accept that she could actually walk away from him without a backward glance. 'Listen to me, Sasha,' he demanded, mollifying the demand with a cajoling tone. 'I miss you. I even miss the baby. The apartment feels empty without you.'

The glib persuasion didn't have the substance to reach past other memories. Sasha eyed him with bleak weariness. 'What you're missing, Tyler, is a convenience you've got used to. Find another woman to look after your needs. The one you tumbled in your studio might oblige.'

It riled him. 'I told you that was a one-off thing.'

'You're free to do whatever you like with whomever you like, Tyler. But not with me and Bonnie.'

His temper flared. 'I came to say I was sorry. What more do you want?'

'Nothing. There's nothing I want from you, except for you to go away and leave us alone.' She held out her hand for the bag. 'Please?'

He ignored the appeal. 'Where do you think you're going to live? You're being totally selfish squatting on your family. They don't have room for you.'

'I intend to find a place of my own.'

'Sure! That will be real easy with a baby in tow and no steady income. You're not thinking straight, Sasha. It's time you stopped sulking and came to your senses.'

'There's no point in this, Tyler. Please give me the bag and let us go.'

'You're being stupidly stubborn. Come back home with me and . . .'

She started walking away without the bag, sick of the argument, sick of everything to do with Tyler, wanting to put him behind her once and for all.

He caught up with her and wrenched one of her arms away from Bonnie, his hand closing around it with biting strength and jerking her around to face him. 'Don't turn your back on me! I came to talk to you.'

'It's no use!' Sasha cried, shocked at being forcibly held and struggling to free herself. Bonnie started screaming at the jolting.

'You're upsetting the kid,' he accused.

'Let me go and she'll be fine. We'll both be fine.'

'You're coming home with me.'

Pulling her after him, denying her any choice, he set off across the park, heading back to where he must have parked his car.

'Stop it, Tyler!' Sasha tried digging her heels in but that caused her to stumble when his relentless forward progress dragged her along with him. 'I don't want to go with you,' she protested.

He didn't so much as slow his pace. 'You're coming whether you like it or not.'

'This won't get you anywhere,' she fiercely promised him, pulling and straining against his iron-tight grip. She was hopelessly incapacitated by the need to hold on to Bonnie who was now screaming at the top of her lungs. Sasha was reduced to pleading. 'Let me go, Tyler. You're hurting me.'

'If you stop being a stubborn mule, you won't get hurt.'

'Let the lady go.'

The command startled both of them. In harnessing all her strength to resist Tyler's caveman tactics, Sasha had forgotten about witnesses. Tyler turned to glare at the man who had suddenly thrust himself into an intervening role. Sasha stared at her self-appointed rescuer in dazed disbelief.

Nathan Parnell had shed his sexy air of relaxed in-
dolence. He looked very big, very strong, and very
determined.

'Butt out, mister,' Tyler snapped at him. 'This is
none of your business.'

Sasha felt a hot surge of humiliation. Being man-
handled in public, and having her helplessness wit-
nessed by Nathan Parnell and his son, was degrading.
She should have handled this confrontation with Tyler more tactfully, although how she could have
stopped him from turning it into an ugly spectacle she
didn't know.

'Let her go or I'll...*break*...your arm.'

The words were loaded with menace. Her uninvited champion stepped forward, obviously prepared
to execute the threat.

The shock of it brought Sasha's miserable train of
thought to an abrupt halt. Why did men have to be
so...so primitive? There was going to be a major
physical confrontation unless she did something to
stop it. And it wasn't necessary.

'It's all right,' she cried. When all was said and
done, she *was* capable of standing up for herself. Tyler didn't mean to do her any physical harm, she was
sure of that.

Nathan Parnell didn't back off but he stopped. 'It
certainly will be,' he said, 'when the gentleman releases you and returns your bag.'

To Sasha's knowledge, Tyler had never been faced
with the threat of physical violence before. With im-
minent danger temporarily averted, shock gave way to

bristling bravado. 'Who the hell do you think you are?' he demanded.

'Parnell. Police officer. Off duty.'

The economy of words reinforced the command of the man and the identification made his stance even more intimidating. It gave Tyler pause for thought. He finally decided discretion was the better part of valour and released Sasha's arm.

Sasha reacted rather than acted. Her self-protective instinct made her step back out of Tyler's reach. Her maternal instinct urged her to soothe Bonnie's alarm. She was too shaken by what had happened to initiate any further resolution to this dreadful scene.

The erstwhile stranger from the sandpit stood his ground, eyeing Tyler as though he were a prime suspect in a murder case.

'You don't understand, Officer,' Tyler blustered. 'This is nothing but a domestic argument.'

'Want to come down to the station and have a friendly chat about it?'

Tyler didn't care for that challenge, either. 'This is ridiculous. Cops everywhere. Isn't there any freedom left in this country?'

'Yes, sir, there is. Freedom for women and children as well as men. Now, if you don't mind, hand over the lady's bag.'

'She has her hands full with the baby. *Our* baby,' Tyler argued.

Nathan Parnell turned to Sasha who was still trying to calm Bonnie. He addressed her quietly, politely, giving no indication that they had met and talked before.

'Would you like me to carry the bag for you, ma'am? I'll give you safe escort to wherever you want to go.'

Sasha felt confused. The authority he had brought to the situation was helping to end it, but she didn't want to get involved with the law. She didn't want to get any further involved with Nathan Parnell, either. He was just as bad as Tyler in wanting a *convenience*, and his he-man display didn't impress her any more than Tyler's did.

'You go with him, Sasha, and you'll never see me again,' Tyler vowed, fuming at having been put in the wrong.

It made up her mind for her. She didn't *want* to see Tyler again. 'Thank you, Officer. I would be grateful for your help.'

He turned back to Tyler and held out his hand. 'The bag please, sir.'

Tyler tossed it at Nathan Parnell's feet, glaring intense hostility at Sasha for her part in his humiliation. 'Don't think you can come crawling back to me. This is it, Sasha. I gave you your chance.'

She made no reply. Nathan Parnell scooped up the bag, stepped between her and Tyler, and took a gentle hold on her elbow to steer her in the direction he wanted her to go. 'If you'll come this way, ma'am . . .'

Sasha hesitated, unsure what she would be getting herself into by going with him. Leaping into the unknown was not her idea of a 'glorious adventure'. Then she remembered his son and realised he must have left the little boy somewhere. Matt should be getting his father's attention.

She moved decisively, submitting to Nathan Parnell's escort, embarrassed by the trouble she hadn't been able to avoid, but relieved to put Tyler behind her. She wondered if it made her a coward, taking the easy way out, but what possible good could it do to continue a post-mortem argument with Tyler? The decision was made. There was no going back.

Matt was, in fact, sitting on the grass a little distance away, gravely watching their approach. Sasha wished he hadn't seen that ugly tussle. It must have disturbed him as much as it had disturbed Bonnie. It rocked children's sense of security when adults fought together.

'Get the rest of your things out of my apartment tomorrow or I'll throw them out,' Tyler shouted after her. 'Your parents will really love having to house all that. They won't have room to move.'

Sasha shuddered, hating the vindictiveness, hating the fact that four years of commitment had come down to this horrible parting.

'Just keep walking. Don't look back,' Nathan Parnell murmured.

She would never have guessed he was a police officer, although he certainly fitted the part, now that she knew. His height, his strong physique, the aura of being in command, unruffled by anything.

'I don't want to make any charge against Tyler,' she said, casting an anxious glance at him.

The compelling blue eyes gently probed hers. 'You don't think he'll trouble you any more?'

Sasha tore her gaze away, fighting a turbulent range of feelings related to his closeness and the caring way he'd looked at her. She was not a little girl in need of his protection, and she was *not* going to succumb to his proposition of a loveless marriage for the sake of having him at her side. He was not a comfort to her at all. He was disruptive and disturbing and the sooner she got away from him, the better.

'I'm quite sure Tyler has wiped his hands of me,' she said stiffly.

She hoped so, anyway. She felt that Tyler had too much ego to leave himself open to another rejection. From now on he would only think bad things about her and consider himself well rid of a relationship that had demanded too much of him anyway. She wondered what explanation he would give to their mutual acquaintances, then decided she didn't care.

None of them had been close friends. Although Joshua, Tyler's business partner, had always been kind. And perceptive. Joshua McDougal had been the only constant associate throughout her four years with Tyler. Social convenience had dictated the pattern of their life. If people weren't *fun*, they were quickly discarded.

Once she had thought Tyler's merry-go-round of people was the answer to all of her dreams. No more loneliness. Lots of people, happy to know her, happy to have her in their company. But it hadn't been real. Not deep-down real. And when it had come to the solid realities of life—responsibilities, commitment, building a solid future together, simply being there when needed—Tyler was, to use Nathan Parnell's words, a dead loss.

She had made the right decision. But it did leave her with some weighty problems, as Tyler had so nastily reminded her.

Matt hopped up to join his father in escorting her and Bonnie from the park. 'I didn't know you were a police officer, Daddy,' he said enquiringly.

It gave Sasha a mental jolt. She had accepted Nathan Parnell's claim without question, but out of the mouths of children came innocent truth.

'When did you become a police officer?' Matt relentlessly pursued the question as children always do.

'When needs must, Matt,' came the quiet reply.

Sasha realised he had supplied what he considered the situation demanded. But who was he really?

The answer exploded through her mind. A man who needed a wife, that was who, and he'd just made the opportunity to proposition her again. Nothing like a white knight to the rescue to soften a woman's heart and mush up her brain. Well, not this woman, thank you very much, Sasha vowed. For the time being, she was through with men.

She stopped walking.

They all stopped walking.

Matt looked up at her. 'My daddy can do anything,' he stated proudly.

'I don't doubt it,' Sasha bit out. She turned to confront the man who considered *when needs must* a good enough reason for arranging matters as he saw fit. 'Do you have anything at all to do with the law, Mr Parnell?'

His craggy, handsome face relaxed into a slow, heart-melting smile. 'I don't mind if you call me Nathan.'

Sasha battled to remain firm in her resistance to any tactics he might employ to persuade her to his way of thinking. 'You didn't answer the question,' she said tersely.

The smile quirked into winsome appeal. The effect was so sexy, Sasha could feel certain nerves quivering in response. 'I practised as a barrister for a while,' he said in a voice that had undoubtedly swayed juries, especially if the jurors were all women.

Sasha refused to be swayed. 'Did you get thrown out for malpractice?' she demanded.

He looked affronted. 'Of course not. I'm a very law-abiding citizen. I like legality. That's the beauty of marriage. Or, at least it would be with a properly drawn-up contract.'

Sasha was not going to get sidetracked on to that issue. Just for once, she was going to pin this man to a proper answer. 'Do you or do you not practise as a barrister now?'

'I do not. I gave it up.'

'Why?'

He shrugged. 'The judges didn't agree with me all the time.'

That didn't come as a surprise. 'I don't agree with you, either,' Sasha asserted.

'Over what?' He looked innocent. 'Have I done something wrong?'

'Threatening bodily harm. I don't believe in violence, Nathan Parnell.'

'Neither do I. None eventuated, did it?'

'No.'

'I rest my case.'

He looked positively smug. It exasperated Sasha into saying, 'I bet you're not always right.'

'My daddy's never wrong,' Matt said, looking up at his father admiringly. 'He told me so.'

'Brainwashed,' Sasha muttered, but she couldn't stop a smile at the precocious little boy.

It was a mistake. Nathan Parnell read it as compliance with their company. 'So, which way is home?' he asked, gesturing for her to indicate direction. 'Matt and I will see you safely to your doorstep. If you like,' he added belatedly, but with a smile that could have buckled her knees if Sasha weren't made of sterner stuff.

It was time to effect the parting of the ways. Nathan Parnell was not the law and Sasha was not about to let him take the law into his own hands any more than he had. She had the distinct feeling that he could twist anything to his purpose, including her if she didn't take herself out of his orbit.

'Thank you, but there's no need.' She looked around. 'Tyler's already gone.'

'What did he mean about having trouble with your parents?'

'I'll have to find a place of my own.' She heaved a rueful sigh. 'It's not easy. Work's been hard to get, and I'm not exactly over-endowed with the world's riches.'

Bonnie had fallen asleep. Sasha shifted her into a more comfortable position against her shoulder then held out her hand. 'May I have my bag now?'

'Sure you don't want me to carry it? It's no trouble.'

She resisted temptation and shook her head. 'I don't have far to walk.'

He handed over the bag. The blue eyes played a last bit of havoc with her pulse-rate as he said, 'Well, good luck with your job-hunting, and I hope you find a decent place to live.'

She met his gaze steadily, resolutely. 'Good luck with finding a wife.'

That was it. She set off and didn't look back, determined to put everything that had happened today behind her. Somewhere, somehow, she would make a good life for herself and Bonnie, even if she never found a man who would love both of them.

'Hold on a moment!'

Nathan Parnell's voice trapped her into looking back. Then the sight of him jogging after her with Matt enjoying a piggy-back ride and happily shouting 'Giddy-up, Daddy,' trapped her into stopping and staring at them. They were both so... heart-tuggingly attractive.

She was still standing like a store dummy when Nathan pulled up beside her. 'Here,' he said, bending over to slip a piece of notepaper into her bag.

'What is it?'

'I just thought of a place where you might get friendly accommodation. I wrote down the woman's name and her phone number. You could try it if you want to. The rent's negotiable.'

'Thanks, but...'

'Don't spoil it.' He grinned. 'That's my two good deeds for the day.'

Then, leaving her with the image of twinkling blue eyes, he was off again, his son bobbing up and down excitedly as his father broke into an obliging canter.

He was, without a doubt, the sexiest man Sasha had ever met.

CHAPTER THREE

SASHA was desperate. It was impossible to stay on with her parents. Their small two-bedroom apartment was uncomfortably overcrowded since she had been forced to retrieve all her possessions before Tyler threw them out. On top of that, a nine-month-old baby did not understand or make allowance for the daily rituals of a retired couple. The unavoidable disruption to the household routine was giving rise to tensions that made life difficult for everyone.

She and Bonnie had to get out.

Day after day Sasha searched for a suitable place but what was affordable was unthinkable: dingy basement bedsits, neighbourhoods where no young child would be safe, dank, sunless rooms that had an unhealthy smell about them. She would have coped if she had only had herself to consider. It was Bonnie's welfare that concerned her. Once again Sasha opened her handbag and took out the piece of paper Nathan Parnell had given her. She hadn't wanted to put herself in a position where she was beholden to him for anything. She had told herself it was better for her if she avoided any possible connection to him. But was it better for Bonnie?

Sasha glanced at her watch. It was almost three o'clock. This time last week she was sitting beside a sandpit in a park, discussing marriage with Nathan Parnell. His image came vividly to mind.

So what if she did run into him again? He hadn't harassed her. He had respected her wishes. And Sasha had promised her mother she would find accommodation as soon as possible. This piece of paper was a chance to nothing. *When needs must,* she thought grimly.

Sasha picked up the telephone and dialled the pencilled numbers with both apprehension and determination, then stared at the woman's name on the notepaper as she waited for the call to be answered.

Five minutes later she had an address in Mosman and an invitation from Marion Bennet to 'come right on over'. However, when Sasha arrived at the recommended 'friendly accommodation', she was thrown into uncertainty about her course of action.

She stared at the magnificent two-storeyed home, unable to believe she had written down the right address. This place had to be worth a fortune, set as it was on harbour frontage and in grounds that had to encompass a couple of acres. Sweeping lawns and long-established gardens gave it an awesome look of prime real estate.

It probably cost a fortune to maintain, as well, Sasha reasoned. Perhaps having tenants helped the owner keep it. In any event, if she had somehow misheard the house number in the street, the best thing to do was find out and ring Marion Bennet again.

With a steadily purposeful step, Sasha made her approach by way of the long gravel driveway. It swept around in a semicircle so visitors could be driven right to the portico that framed the entrance to the house. Sasha couldn't help feeling like an intruder as she walked up and pressed the doorbell.

To her startled surprise, she heard it play a few bars of 'Jingle Bells'. It reminded her that it was the last week in November and all the shops were full of Christmas cheer. She hoped she could make Bonnie's first Christmas a happy one.

One of the double doors opened. Sasha was faced with a woman of similar age to her mother, grey hair neatly groomed, her rather buxom figure comfortably dressed in a loose-fitting top and casual cotton trousers. Her hazel eyes were bright with interest as they swept over Sasha in quick appraisal.

Sasha had dressed professionally in a navy skirt and white blouse, stockings, low-heeled court shoes. Her long hair was wound into a smooth top-knot and she had applied a light make-up to give her face some colour. She hoped she looked like a sensible, responsible and trustworthy person.

'Mrs Bennet?' she asked on a slightly anxious note.

The woman gave her a friendly smile. 'That's me. And you must be Miss Redford.'

'Yes.' Sasha smiled in relief. She had the right address after all.

But it still didn't look right when Mrs Bennet stood back and waved her forward. The foyer extended in a wonderful pattern of mosaic tiles to a magnificent polished cedar staircase that curved up to the top floor.

'We could go up that way, but there's another staircase by the kitchen that you'll find handier,' Mrs Bennet explained, leading Sasha into a side passage. 'I'm afraid there's no private entrance to the nursery and nanny's quarters.'

Apparently that was the accommodation for rent. Feeling somewhat intimidated by her surroundings, Sasha simply nodded.

'I'll give you your bearings as we go,' Mrs Bennet continued. 'The formal rooms are on our right, the TV- and breakfast-rooms on our left.'

She opened doors as they passed them, giving Sasha a glimpse of luxurious living on a scale she had never met before. The ceilings had to be at least fourteen feet high, and the furniture was out of this world.

Between the breakfast-room and the kitchen was a lobby that served the second staircase. This was much less grand than the first, the treads not so wide, and there were three landings as it angled around the wall to the upper floor.

As she followed Mrs Bennet's steady climb, Sasha had the sinking feeling that, however negotiable the rent was, this setting virtually precluded its being within her means. She should bring the matter up now to save wasting her own and Mrs Bennet's time, but the temptation to see what was being offered was irresistible.

'This is the nursery.'

Sasha was ushered into a bright, airy room, predominantly lemon and white, and containing every possible facility a mother and baby might need: storage cupboards, shelves, a changing table, a cot, a comfortable rocking-chair.

The nanny's quarters were equally spacious and complete. The bed-sitting-room had all the facilities and comforts provided in a top motel: a double bed, writing desk, small lounge suite, table and chairs, television, telephone.

Sasha couldn't even dream that the asking rent for this marvellous place would be in her capacity to pay. She tried to find some fault so she could retreat from the situation without loss of dignity. It was difficult to find a fault, but she came up with one.

'I need a private telephone line,' she said.

Mrs Bennet nodded a ready acceptance. 'I'm sure that can be arranged.'

'I need it for my business,' Sasha said defensively.

'Do you sell things from home?' Mrs Bennet enquired.

'No. I find things.'

She saw the incomprehension in the older woman's eyes and explained further.

'I find whatever people want found. It started with research for family trees, finding long-lost relatives, beneficiaries for wills. But it branched into tracking down family heirlooms and other things. The provenance of paintings or other works of art. Finding the owner of some rarity that someone wants to buy. Mostly people don't know where to start or where to go for the information they want.'

'What an interesting occupation! Do you get many people wanting your services?'

'Not too many lately. But I do use the phone a lot when I'm working.'

'It must save you considerable legwork,' Mrs Bennet said appreciatively, then dismissed the issue, leading Sasha through another doorway. 'I'm afraid the kitchenette is more or less limited to serving a baby's needs than cooking meals, but of course you'll have free use of the kitchen downstairs.'

It looked more than fine to Sasha. It was sheer luxury after what she had seen this week. It provided a small refrigerator, kitchen sink, a microwave oven, ample storage cupboards, and a benchtop with several power points.

Then there was the en-suite bathroom. It contained a bath for the baby as well as a separate shower stall if she preferred that herself.

Satisfied that Sasha had seen all there was to see, Mrs Bennet led her back into the nursery and pointed out one of the windows. 'The swimming-pool is fenced for safety. You're welcome to use it as you please. And the grounds. As I said, you don't have a private entrance but we tend to live as a family here. No one will mind your coming or going through the house, front or back entrance.'

It was time to bite the bullet on the question of rent. The case was hopeless but Sasha had to know. 'Mrs Bennet, you've been wonderfully kind showing me around, and I'd love to live here, but I don't know if I can afford it. If you'd give me some idea . . .'

The older woman smiled. 'Well, that's up to you, my dear. These rooms are simply being wasted with no one in them. What would you like to pay?'

It put Sasha on the spot. She wished a definite figure had been stated. Much easier to say no than to
have to reveal the truth of her situation. Her mind
went through a feverish calculation, stretching her
means to the uppermost limit of what she might be
able to reasonably pay each week without running into
trouble.

'I don't have much work at the present moment, but
I do have a bit of money put aside,' she explained. 'I
can afford...' It was so inadequate, it would barely
cover the cost of a bedsitter in the poorest part of
Sydney.

'Go on,' said Mrs Bennet helpfully, her eyes soft
with sympathy.

It seemed insulting to offer so little. In a voice she
hardly recognised as her own, Sasha spoke the fateful
words. 'A hundred dollars a week.' She could feel the
blood burning through her cheeks. She turned aside,
not wanting to face the reply, feeling humiliated and
defeated.

'I'm afraid that won't do, my dear. I'm afraid that
won't do at all.'

Mrs Bennet had seemed such a nice person, but
making her propose a figure that exposed how desti-
tute she was...it was belittling and demeaning. 'I'm
sorry to have wasted your time,' Sasha said tone-
lessly, and headed for the door.

'What you are offering is far, far, far too much.'

It made Sasha pause. Was she hallucinating? Was
her hearing defective today? She could not conceal the
surprise she felt, nor did she attempt to hide it or dis-
guise it as she swung around in disbelief. 'I must have

misheard. I thought you said I offered too much money.'

Mrs Bennet looked puzzled. 'Didn't Mr Parnell tell you?'

Completely confused about what was going on, Sasha repeated what she had been told. 'He said the rent was negotiable.'

'So it is, my dear, but under the terms of the will of the late Seagrave Dunworthy there is a *caveat* on the property that prevents any room, or any number of rooms, from being let or rented beyond a certain price. The rental that may be charged up to that maximum figure is negotiable, but if the owner were to accept any figure above that price, then the owner would be liable to litigation which could effectively cause a disinheritance and loss of ownership.'

Sasha's professional curiosity was piqued. In the course of her work she had read a lot of strange and eccentric wills, but none like this. 'Are you sure of your facts? I've never heard of such a thing.'

'That's what I've been told, and I have no reason to disbelieve it,' Mrs Bennet assured her.

Sasha hesitated fractionally, then plunged to the heart of the matter. 'Then how much is the maximum figure that can be charged for a room or a set of rooms?'

'Five guineas a week.'

Reading old documents had made Sasha familiar with this unit of currency. It predated the introduction of decimal currency in 1966, and its real vogue was in the nineteenth century, although it had still been used in auctioneering circles, and particularly the horse-racing industry, up to a couple of generations ago. She did the mental calculation of converting this old coinage into pounds and shillings, and then into dollars and cents.

'That works out at ten dollars and fifty cents.'

'That is correct.' Without the slightest loss of aplomb, Mrs Bennet explained the position so that Sasha could appreciate it properly. 'You can negoti- ate any figure you like for the rent, up to a maximum of ten dollars fifty.'

Sasha still couldn't make herself believe it. 'The will must be very old to have been written in such terms,' she said, driven to question the validity of what she was being told.

'I don't have any information on that,' Mrs Bennet replied, looking totally unconcerned by such a con- sideration.

'Surely with the effect of inflation...'

'I've been led to believe there is no mention of the effects of inflation in the will of the late and highly esteemed Seagrave Dunworthy.'

'Oh!'

Sasha didn't know where to go from there. Faced with the unbelievable that was apparently irrefutable, her mind went into numb stasis.

Mrs Bennet eventually jolted her out of it. 'Really, my dear, you must make up your mind whether to take the rooms or not,' she said in a kindly but matter-of- fact voice. 'I do have other things to do.'

'Yes. Well, of course I'll take them. In the circum- stances.'

However dubious the circumstances were, Sasha told herself she would be stupid to look a gift horse in the mouth. Particularly in *her* circumstances.

'In that case, I must tell you now that the terms of the agreement are very specific,' Mrs Bennet said with an air of serious warning. 'Firstly, any benefactor of the revered Seagrave Dunworthy must speak of him in the most laudable terms. Otherwise they may lose the benefits conferred on them by the will.'

'Oh, I'll certainly do that,' Sasha said with feeling. 'He must have been a wonderful man.'

'Highly esteemed,' Mrs Bennet agreed. 'And secondly, the rental conditions are very precise. The money must be paid each Friday morning, after nine o'clock, and before the grandfather clock in the entrance hall chimes the twelfth stroke of the twelfth hour at midday.'

The eccentricity of this instruction seemed to add a ring of substance to the rest of Seagrave Dunworthy's will. 'I can't pay in advance?' Sasha asked.

'Definitely not.'

'Ten dollars fifty,' Sasha repeated in dazed bemusement.

'For convenience, ten is better,' Mrs Bennet advised. 'Then we don't have to worry about change.'

'Ten,' Sasha agreed, wondering if she had fallen through the looking glass like Alice. 'I get all this for ten dollars.'

'Well, if you'd like to negotiate...'

'No, no. Ten dollars is fine. I'll pay it first thing on Friday morning.'

'After nine o'clock,' Mrs Bennet reminded her. 'Now let's go downstairs and I'll give you duplicate keys for the front and back doors. Then you can move in whenever you like.'

'It will be tomorrow.'

'That's fine, dear.'

Sasha was in such a daze that it wasn't until Mrs Bennet was escorting her to the front door that a niggle of curiosity slithered into her mind. 'Does Mr Parnell know about the terms of Seagrave Dunworthy's will?'

'Oh, yes, dear. Mr Parnell is a lawyer. He explained all the terms of the will to me.'

A man of many parts, Sasha thought. Retired barrister, white knight, boy scout, the sexiest man she had ever met, and what else?

'I don't know what we would have done without Mr Parnell,' Mrs Bennet continued. 'We ran into terrible trouble. My husband was robbed of his business, although we couldn't prove it in court. We lost everything: our livelihood, the roof over our heads, all the money we had saved. We had nowhere to turn until Mr Parnell suggested this place and got us settled here.'

'He did that for you, too?' Sasha mentally added Good Samaritan to the list.

'Such a kind man.' Mrs Bennet opened the front door and smiled at Sasha. It seemed to be a 'welcome to the family' kind of smile. 'My husband will help you carry your belongings in tomorrow if you need a hand, dear. I'm sure you'll be very happy here.'

'Thank you.'

It seemed ungrateful to linger, taking up more of Mrs Bennet's time, but the memory of all those grand rooms prompted one last question. 'Does anyone else live here besides you and Mr Bennet?'

'Why, of course, dear. I thought you knew. Mr Parnell lives here.'

CHAPTER FOUR

BY EIGHT o'clock on Sunday night, Sasha had moved herself and Bonnie into the Mosman mansion. She was unpacked and as settled as she was ever likely to be in this household. She didn't know how long her occupancy was going to last, but she was going to make the most of it while she could.

Bonnie was fast asleep in the nursery. Sasha had the luxury of the nanny's quarters to herself. She took a long, hot shower, pampered herself by putting on her peacock blue satin robe, then brushed her hair as she made a critical assessment of herself in the vanity mirror.

She had never been called pretty. Tyler had said she was elegant. Fine bones, a long neck and the straight fall of black hair to below her shoulderblades had been her main attractions to him. She wondered what Nathan Parnell saw in her, apart from her skin. She did have fine skin, but she had always thought of it as pale, not creamy, and tonight there were signs of stress and fatigue under her eyes. The last few weeks had not been easy.

Sasha put down the hairbrush and strolled into the kitchenette. A cup of coffee, then she would see what was on TV. She switched on the percolator, feeling a deep sense of satisfaction in not having to consider anyone but herself.

She hadn't seen Nathan Parnell all day. Mrs Bennet had told her he and Matt had gone visiting; Sasha didn't ask with whom or where. She was determined not to show any interest in him. But Mrs Bennet had told her other items of interest.

She and her husband rented the servants' quarters on the other side of the main kitchen. Nathan Parnell employed them as his housekeeper and handyman. This very convenient arrangement gave rise to grave suspicions in Sasha's mind.

Nathan Parnell liked convenience. He also used the law to suit himself. Seagrave Dunworthy's highly eccentric will could very well be an invention of Nathan Parnell's fertile mind. It had brought him the Bennets, who obviously served him well, believing they were the recipients of remarkable good fortune. With the same good fortune extended to Sasha, he might be counting on getting himself a compliant wife.

If so, he could think again. Desperate situations required desperate solutions, but Sasha couldn't believe her situation would become so desperate she would consider marriage in any circumstances to Nathan Parnell.

The more Sasha pondered her position here, the more it seemed to her that it didn't matter whether Seagrave Dunworthy was an authentic person or not. All she had to do was believe in him implicitly and esteem him so highly that no one could ever fault her on that score. The terms of his will not only allowed her to live here cheaply, but also independently of Nathan Parnell's good will or humour. As long as she paid her rent within the required time on Fridays, Nathan Parnell could have nothing to complain about.

The percolator boiled.

There was a knock on the door.

'Come in,' she called, wondering what Mrs Bennet had forgotten to tell her this time.

Sasha poured coffee into her cup, heard the door open; then realised several moments passed without a word being spoken. Surprised into looking for the reason, Sasha lifted her head and was abruptly jolted out of her complacency. Marion Bennet was not her visitor at all. It was Nathan Parnell.

He stood by the opened door, apparently as transfixed by the sight of her as Sasha was by him. He was dressed in navy trousers and a white shirt, yet Sasha was instantly assailed by a sense of dangerous intimacy and a heart-choking awareness of dangerous virility.

Her mind registered shirt buttons left undone, a deep V of tanned chest with a sprinkle of dark curls, rolled-up shirt-sleeves, muscular forearms, the damp sheen of hair freshly washed, electric blue eyes that sent sizzling sensations pulsing to sensitive places.

She was suddenly, flamingly conscious of her nakedness under the silk of her robe. Her skin sprang alive with awareness. Her nipples tightened. She searched frantically for something to say, anything to disrupt the current of serious sexuality flowing between them.

'I thought it was Marion Bennet.'

He didn't seem to hear. She needed something less obvious, more earth-shaking. Nothing came to mind.

'How striking you look in that vibrant blue.' His deep baritone voice seemed to throb through her. His mouth slowly curved into a whimsical smile that was somehow loaded with sensuality. 'I don't suppose you're wearing it for me.'

'No.'

'What a waste.'

Sasha desperately gathered her wits, determined not to be drawn into anything she didn't want. 'I have to thank you for suggesting this accommodation,' she said, trying for a neighbourly attitude.

His smile broadened. 'Your gratitude would be better directed to Seagrave Dunworthy. I was merely the intermediary. A cup of coffee will be repayment enough.'

'I was getting ready for bed.'

'So was I.' The blue eyes twinkled wickedly. 'And I thought of you.'

'As an afterthought of the day's activities?'

Sasha laughed. It was the only way to break the tug of his attraction and hopefully lift the conversation to a lighter note.

'The day's activities concerned you. I went to see Hester Wingate.'

'Is that someone else who's left some kind of marvellous will from which I can benefit?'

'No, but she's working on it. And she wants your services.'

'In what capacity?'

'Marion told me your profession was finding things. Hester is eager to employ your expertise.'

'You got me a job?'

'To make sure you could pay the rent.'

And keep me here, Sasha reasoned. Nathan Parnell was irrepressible, and probably ten steps ahead of her. She had no doubt that behind the twinkling eyes was a determined will to have his own way. He was not shy of playing any trick to get it, either. What have I let myself in for? Sasha wondered, then tried again to assert some control over the situation.

'Don't you think it's rather improper to visit me in my bedroom? Is this what I'm to expect?'

He shrugged. 'You're free to evict me if you want. But then you wouldn't know about the job.'

He had an indisputable point there. She needed work. She also needed this accommodation. But she didn't need a husband who didn't love her and Bonnie.

'Does a cup of coffee cover that favour as well, or are you expecting more?' she asked in dry challenge.

'I like mine black and two sugars,' he said, and promptly shut the door.

'Sit at the table. I'll bring it over,' Sasha instructed, wary of allowing him to set a cosier scene. As it was, he hadn't really answered her question and she wanted some firm distance between them. Like a good solid slab of wood.

'Did Bonnie settle down OK?' he asked affably, lessening her tension by doing as he was told.

'Sound asleep,' she replied.

'So is Matt,' he said with satisfaction.

Which instantly put the thought of *bed* in Sasha's mind. She fought off the idea that Nathan was thinking their children were conveniently accounted for. He had gained admittance to her room, but it was more than ten steps to her bed and she was definitely not going to give him any encouragement whatsoever in that direction.

Having surreptitiously checked that her robe was securely wrapped around her, Sasha took both cups of coffee to the table and settled herself on the chair opposite his.

'Now tell me what this job is about,' she invited, intent on keeping strictly to business.

His mouth twitched. 'Muck-raking.'

'Then I'm sorry you've wasted your time on my account. I'm not into scandal or anything defamatory that would hurt other people.'

She placed her elbows on the table, picked up her cup, lifted it to her mouth and sipped, hoping he would take the hint that the reason for him being with her was now limited to coffee-drinking.

He grinned openly, undeterred by dismissals or hints. 'Hester Wingate is ninety-two years old. Or, at least, that's what she admits to. She's probably older. She's the last of her tribe. All her friends, brothers, sisters have passed away. There are a few old scores she never got to settle. But that doesn't deter Hester. She wants the information for the *other side*.'

'What other side?'

'The vast beyond. The next life. I'm not quite sure how Hester sees the *other side*—whether they're all going to be together in heaven, or hell, or somewhere entirely different. But whatever it is, Hester wants to be prepared for them who done her wrong in this life.'

Sasha couldn't help being amused. 'Well, that does rather change the situation,' she conceded. 'You mean she wants to muck-rake in the far past about people who are dead and gone.'

'Precisely. Every last skeleton in every last closet. Nothing to be overlooked.'

'Can she afford my services?'

'What do you charge?'

Sasha hesitated. She really needed a good substantial job. If the old lady was a pensioner, it was unlikely she could pay much, but anything was better than nothing in her present straitened circumstances, and often one job led to another.

'The accepted rate is twenty-five dollars an hour plus expenses, but most people can't afford too many hours at that rate,' she said with rueful honesty. 'Usually, because I can't get much done in an hour, I put in a couple of hours for every one I charge.'

'Well, that's one way to get rich,' he drily remarked.

It made Sasha feel defensive, which drove her to an aggressive reply. 'It takes a long time to dig up real substance.'

'I'm sure it does,' he agreed. His eyes twinkled with infectious good humour, completely defusing any offence given. 'Hester has a lot of old scores to settle. If you're any good at giving her what she wants, you may end up being fully employed for years.'

The prospect of full employment for a while sounded too good to be true. Sasha's suspicions were aroused. 'Precisely who is this Hester Wingate and what connection do you have with her?'

'I'll take you to meet her if you're interested in the job. I do her legal work.'

'Then the law is still your profession.'

He shook his head. 'I only do it for Hester because no one else would put up with her.'

'A favour, you might say,' Sasha prompted.

'Very much so.'

And a favour for a favour seemed very much down Nathan Parnell's alley. Sasha's suspicions moved up a notch. 'She sounds extremely eccentric.' And possibly primed for the part by her legal consultant.

Nathan rolled his eyes. 'Believe me, you'll earn your money. I've redrafted her will at least twenty times. She had another codicil for me today.'

Another will. Another fertile invention by Nathan Parnell? 'Nothing could be more eccentric than Seagrave Dunworthy's will,' Sasha posed, wanting to see if he reacted to the connection.

He gave her a crooked smile. 'Want to bet on that?'

Maybe it was all true. Sasha had to admit to being intrigued by the prospect of investigating the situation. Besides, a job was a job, and, if she was promptly paid for the work she did, what did it matter if Nathan Parnell was behind it? As with this accommodation, as long as she believed everything was genuine, there was nothing for her to worry about.

'Where does Hester Wingate live?' she asked, getting down to practicalities.

'Church Point. In actual fact, I am commanded to bring you to her in time for morning tea tomorrow.

You are to bring your baby with you.' His eyes made an eloquent appeal. 'It would save me a lot of trouble if you agree.'

'You don't mind being ordered around?'

He sighed. 'I find it easier to fit in with Hester than not to.'

Despite her suspicions, Sasha was amused. The idea of a little old lady getting the better of Nathan Parnell was so unlikely, she wanted to see it for herself. 'It's very kind of you,' she said.

'I take it you're agreeable to the plan?'

'It couldn't be more agreeable,' she assured him. 'And I'm very grateful to you for thinking of me.'

'It was no hardship.'

His eyes locked on to hers, telling her it was a pleasure, the kind of pleasure a man took in doing something for a woman who was of keen personal interest to him.

Sasha's stomach quivered. She forced her eyes down. Her cup was still in her hands. She drank the coffee as though it were a life-saving necessity.

He picked up his cup. He had long, lean fingers, neatly manicured nails. Was he the kind of lover who would take and give sensual pleasure, tracing exquisite patterns on her skin with those fingers? Sasha caught her breath at the sheer eroticism of her thoughts. She had to get Nathan Parnell out of here before something inappropriate occurred. She waited until he finished his coffee, then tried to bring their business together to a quick conclusion.

'What time should we leave in the morning?'

'Can you be ready by nine-thirty?'

'Yes.' She stood up and gave him a weary smile. 'But I do need a good night's sleep.'

'I'll leave you to it.'

To Sasha's intense relief he rose to his feet without any attempt to prolong this encounter. She led the way to the door, opened it, then steadied herself to bid him goodnight.

'Thanks for all your help, Nathan.'

He paused beside her, his vivid blue eyes capturing hers with concentrated purpose. He was too close, disturbingly close.

'Would passion suffice?' he asked.

She felt his hands on her waist and knew he meant to kiss her. Probably he wanted more. Without a wife...

Her heart clenched, hit turmoil, and shattered into chaos. She shouldn't let him...she shouldn't...but a kiss was just a kiss. She could stop it at that. A kiss didn't commit her to anything. There were many reasons for giving him this little pleasure. He'd done a lot for her. He wanted it. And he was the sexiest man she had ever met.

In mind-spinning fascination she watched his mouth coming towards hers. She hadn't kissed anyone but Tyler for over four years, and in recent times there had been little feeling left in that. Mostly desperation. Often resignation. But that was gone now, and she was free to please herself, free to accept a kiss from another man, and she wanted to know what it would be like.

His lips moved lightly over hers, tempting, tantalising, encouraging her to respond. No demand. No pressure. Nothing to be frightened of. Her hands slid up to his shoulders, allowing him the freedom to gather her closer. He didn't. It was a long, slow kiss, one of sensual invitation and exploration, caressing away Sasha's thoughts. She went with him, following every step, entranced with the journey of escalating sensation.

A sigh, mingled with regret and satisfaction, whispered from her lips when he ended the kiss. The pleasure of it still lingered in her mouth. She wanted to taste more, and very quickly.

'Stolen kisses are the sweetest,' he murmured against her ear.

She opened her eyes and stared dazedly at him, wondering if he had felt anything special. 'You call that passion?' she taunted, piqued that he was still in control of himself.

'No. I call *this* passion.'

She saw the flare of desire in his eyes. Then his mouth claimed hers again, and his arms enfolded her, and his hands moulded her body to his, and there was no holding back. No control. Not for either of them.

Precisely how their passionate immersion in each other came to an end was a hazy area in Sasha's mind afterwards. Had they both pulled back, not having expected to feel so much? A mutual inter-reaction? Or had Nathan sensed some hesitation on her part, and given her the benefit of any doubt in her mind?

She heard him say, 'Tomorrow,' in a deep husky voice. There was a gentle disengagement, his hands steadying her before slipping away. Then he was gone.

She headed for her bed, barely aware of what she was doing, automatically switching off lights. She stretched out luxuriously between the sheets, her body still tingling with the sensations Nathan had aroused. She ran her fingers lightly over her lips. They weren't swollen, but they still felt highly sensitive.

Nathan Parnell had certainly delivered passion. She could very easily have ended up in bed with him. He had been fully aroused, urgently aroused, and the hard pressure of his need against her stomach had been like some wild aphrodisiac, triggering a sense of elation through her mind and a pounding excitement through her body. She had lost all track of any common sense in the dizzying pleasure of feeling wanted by such a desirable man. She had wanted him, too.

In retrospect, she was glad they had stopped where they had. Plunging into physical intimacy would have given her an involvement that had gone far too far, far too fast. Passion was not love. And it wouldn't suffice to hold a marriage together, either. She would have to disabuse Nathan of that idea.

On the other hand, he was a very intriguing man, attractive on many levels, and Sasha didn't want to discourage him completely from pursuing a relationship with her. It might lead to much more than passion, given time to get to know each other properly. Thanks to him, they were ideally placed to do precisely that.

A pleasurable little bubble of anticipation danced around Sasha's mind. Seagrave Dunworthy was a marvellous man. Hester Wingate sounded as though she was an equally marvellous woman. Nathan Parnell might rearrange his ideas on what made a marvellous marriage. Who knew what tomorrow might bring?

CHAPTER FIVE

SASHA woke the next morning to what seemed like a different world. She could hear Bonnie babbling her contentment with whatever was in her line of vision in the nursery. A new home, a new job, and a new life, Sasha thought, and with a zest for getting on with it she sprang out of bed and headed for the bathroom.

Today she was going to look as good as she could. She would wash and blow-dry her hair into shiny sleekness. She would wear her fashionable, lipstick pink coat-dress and black patent high heels. She would dress Bonnie in her best clothes. There was a lot to do before she met up with Nathan at nine-thirty.

Time flew by. She had Bonnie strapped securely into her carrycot ready to carry downstairs when Nathan appeared at the nursery door. Sasha had left it open to facilitate her exit.

'Need some assistance?'

'I was just coming,' she replied, quickly scanning his face to see how he felt about what had happened between them last night.

The look he gave her came from a man who knew what he liked and had no inhibitions about showing it. His eyes danced appreciatively over her face and the long gleaming tresses of her hair, then simmered reminiscently over the curves of her figure and the shapeliness of her stockinged legs. The pleasure and satisfaction in his smile spread a warm glow under Sasha's skin.

'I've never seen any woman look so superb in that colour,' he said with flattering directness.

'I'm glad you think so.'

Dressed in a silky three-piece blue-grey suit, with a blue and gold tie to set it off, Nathan Parnell looked a very distinguished man of considerable class, devastatingly handsome, and master of his world. But not master of hers, Sasha swiftly amended, not unless she could feel it was absolutely right.

'Red might be more stunning on you,' he said consideringly.

She laughed in self-conscious pleasure at his interest in her appearance. 'I do have a red satin evening dress but I didn't think it was appropriate for the occasion.'

'I shall make sure an occasion arises.'

Excitement welled up in Sasha. He really meant to pursue a relationship with her. Or was he thinking she would make a suitably ornamental wife, as well as a desirable woman in his bed?

'Where's Matt this morning?' she asked, remembering he didn't come unattached.

'At playschool. It gives him the chance to mix with other children.'

He stepped forward to bend over Bonnie in her carrycot, smiling down at Sasha's baby and letting her curl her little fingers around one of his. Bonnie blew a few bubbles to show her appreciation of his attention.

A good father, Sasha thought.

He picked up the carrycot and the accompanying holdall, lifting his heart-tugging smile to Sasha. 'Ready?'

'Yes, thank you.'

She followed him downstairs, resolving to find out more about him on their drive to Church Point. All she really had was a stack of impressions, some of them well-founded but hardly what one might call solid information.

A white BMW was parked at the front steps. She watched him place Bonnie's cot on the back seat and secure it properly. He saw Sasha settled into the front passenger seat, waiting until she had her safety belt fastened before closing the door. It made her extremely aware of his physical closeness, and when he joined her in the car she couldn't help giving him a cursory look, matching his body against her memory of how it had felt pressed against her last night.

His eyes suddenly caught hers. For a moment there was a simmering promise in them, as though he, too, was remembering what they had shared. Then he turned his attention to starting the car and getting it on the road. Sasha sat very still, her heart zipping up and down a scale like a hammer on a xylophone. Nathan Parnell intended it to happen between them. It was only a question of *when*.

It couldn't be today, Sasha thought, not with Bonnie present. A sense of shock rippled through her. Too far, too fast, her mind hammered in swift reaction.

She had never been a promiscuous person. Despite her discontent with Tyler, she had remained faithful to him, and never once fancied any other man. Casual sex did not appeal to her. She wanted more than temporary passion. She wanted the deep, forever kind of love.

'When you're not drawing up codicils for Hester Wingate's will, what do you do?' she asked, determined that their relationship progress how she wanted it to progress. If it was to progress at all.

He slanted her a twinkling smile. 'I play computer games.'

She sighed her exasperation. 'I mean, how do you exist?'

'Most people would say very comfortably. I guess it depends on what your ambitions and priorities are.'

'Are you saying you're retired from work?'

'No. But I am in a position to choose what I do.'

'Which is?'

'Do you like diamonds, Sasha?'

She couldn't see the relevance of this question but she automatically looked down at her left hand, thinking of the engagement ring she had once hoped for from Tyler. 'As much as most women, I guess,' she answered, striving for a careless note. Was he thinking he could buy her with a diamond ring?

'There's an exhibition in the city. The best of the coloured diamonds from the Argyle Mine in the Kimberleys. The pinks are my favourite.'

She glanced at him in surprise. 'You like pink diamonds?'

'Fabulous. Would you like to see them? I'll show you how I protect them. With a computer game.'

'I'd like that.'

She couldn't imagine what he had to do with diamonds, nor what he did to protect them, but she wasn't about to miss out on full enlightenment. With this kind of car, and the classy suit he was wearing, Nathan Parnell was not exactly on government welfare. Nor were there many people so wealthy that they could afford to wind down and work at their own convenience at such a young age.

'How old are you?' she asked.

'Thirty-four.'

'Are you anti-social?'

He gave her an amused look. 'Do I act and talk as though I'm anti-social?'

'No,' she conceded, and thought how paradoxical he was. Why hadn't he found a woman of his own class to marry? Why pick on her, a stranger he'd met by complete chance in a park? Perhaps she should simply adopt his attitude of 'wait and see', instead of asking questions. Besides, she rather liked the surprises he sprang on her. It made life very interesting.

She turned her mind to the fast approaching interview with Hester Wingate. She had never been to Church Point, but knew it was on the innermost edge of Pittwater, a playground for sailing boats and other water sports. It was protected from the sea by the long Palm Beach peninsula, and renowned for its wealthy and prestigious marinas and yacht club. It was an expensive area in which to live.

Because of Hester Wingate's age, Sasha expected her to live in an old-style home. She was staggered when Nathan turned his car into the driveway of what could only be called a modern and luxurious villa, a huge pink and white construction that had two levels of Mediterranean-style verandas overlooking the sparkling expanse of water. The grounds were a luxuriant mass of tropical ferns and palms, hibiscus and frangipani trees. A gardener was raking up dead leaves.

'She can definitely afford twenty-five dollars an hour,' Sasha said with satisfaction.

Nathan laughed. 'Try thirty or forty. She'll respect your expertise more.'

They alighted from the car. Bonnie was fast asleep. Nathan took the carrycot. Sasha collected the baby's bag. They started up a massive concrete staircase that curved up to the lower-level veranda.

Nathan caught Sasha's hand. 'For courage,' he said, his smile a promise of support.

'Is she so formidable?' Sasha asked, inwardly marvelling over how good an act of friendliness could feel. Friendship was more important than passion.

'Depends on her mood. But, yes, she can be difficult.'

Sasha hoped Hester Wingate was disposed to like her. She wanted this job. It could mean a lot to her.

They reached the veranda. A huge variety of exotic plants in exotic pots suggested the owner was a collector of the unusual. Nathan led Sasha to a white aluminium dining setting which was positioned to catch the breeze off the water and a steady stream of sunshine. He placed Bonnie's cot on the table.

'I'll give Hester a call.'

He was very familiar with this house, Sasha thought, watching him slide open a set of glass doors and stroll into a vast living-room. It made her wonder once more if the job with Hester Wingate was a genuine one, or a contrivance agreed upon between Nathan Parnell and an old and trusted friend who could afford any indulgence.

Sasha dropped the holdall on one of the chairs and waited. She took several deep breaths to calm herself. Voices alerted her to their approach. The image Sasha had conjured up in her mind of Hester Wingate was blasted to pieces by a completely different reality.

She was little. She was old. She used a walking stick. But that was definitely the only concession to her ninety-two years, and even the walking stick was an elegant ivory and silver fashion statement.

Her hair was like a finely spun candy-floss confection in a silvery mauve colour. She wore a flowing caftan that shimmered with pinks and blues and aqua. Her eyes were a fascinating light blue, twinkling with lively interest, radiating energy. She stopped in the doorway between the living-room and the veranda and gave Sasha a thorough once-over that might have been rude from anyone else, but quite clearly Hester Wingate assumed it her right to examine guests as she pleased.

'I see,' she said, nodding vigorously. 'So this is the girl who is creating all the fuss.'

Sasha felt she had been catalogued under the wrong identification. She looked to Nathan for guidance.

'Under the will of...' Nathan began blandly.

'Don't pay any attention to him,' Hester commanded. 'Young women are meant to create a fuss. To leave a trail of devastated men in their wake. It's the only thing young women can do effectively.'

But it wasn't true. Not in this case. Unless Nathan had made a fuss about giving her the job.

'Are you clever?' Hester fired the question point-blank.

Sasha was at a loss as to how to answer. Fortunately Hester Wingate didn't require a reply. She appeared to be adept at holding conversations where only she spoke.

'It's a matter of bloodlines,' she said, and stepped over to the table to examine Bonnie. 'Never buy a horse without examining its bloodlines.' She shot a piercing look at Sasha. 'Do you understand that?'

'I have no intention of either buying or selling a horse,' Sasha said weakly. 'I've come about a job.'

'Now there's a child anyone might be proud of,' Hester declared, giving Bonnie her nod of approval before turning the full blast of her attention back to Sasha. 'Is she healthy?'

'Yes.'

'Are you healthy?'

'Yes, I'm healthy, too.'

Her eyes skated down Sasha's body. 'I like to see a woman with good wide hips. Saves a lot of problems.'

Sasha burned. This was going too far. It made her feel she was being regarded as a brood mare about to be put to stud.

'I whinny when I'm given oats for breakfast,' she said, flashing a withering glare at Nathan Parnell for his part in subjecting her to this absurd farce.

'Spirited,' Hester remarked as though Sasha had scored another high mark. 'Let me see you smile.'

'Madam, I must protest . . .'

'I will not work with either unpleasant or eccentric people. They are the two types of people I cannot abide.'

Sasha couldn't help smiling at the whimsy of this speech. Hester Wingate appeared to be both.

'Good teeth,' Hester said with satisfaction. 'My dear, you have passed all the tests so far. You have the job.'

'Thank you.' Sasha had nothing else to say. She didn't know if she had just been approved of as a suitable wife for Nathan Parnell, or as a suitable person to be in Hester Wingate's employ.

'Do sit down and make yourself comfortable, dear.' It was another autocratic command. 'Nathan, set the baby down just inside the door so we'll hear her when she wakes. Jane will bring morning tea in a few minutes.'

Sasha eyed Nathan with dark suspicion. He must have told Hester Wingate about his intention to enter a marriage of convenience and that Sasha was his selected candidate for the position of his wife. This job was almost certainly bogus, a means of persuading her that supplying solutions to needs was better than a love match.

His response to her look was to spread his hands in a gesture of innocence, and roll his eyes to suggest Hester was beyond his control.

Sasha didn't believe that for a second, but there was no profit in walking out in high dudgeon. Better to bite her tongue and sit this out. She could decide later what she was going to do.

Hester took the chair at the head of the table. When they were all settled, she reached over and patted Sasha's hand. 'I hope you don't mind, my dear, but at my age I don't have time for social chit-chat. Get on with the job. That's what I say. I take it you agree.'

'Definitely,' Sasha agreed with mixed feelings.

'When we start I'll take you to the history room. I've collected all the family bibles. All have been tampered with.' Hester paused for effect. 'It's a sad day when it's no longer possible to believe in the dates entered in a bible.'

'What do you want me to do about it?' Sasha asked.

'Find out the truth. Dig up the dirt. Nail everybody that can be nailed.'

'Is that all you want?' With a list of names and dates, it was an easy matter to check them. There wouldn't be many hours involved.

The old lady eyed her warily. 'I hope you're not suffering from false confidence, my dear. You are dealing with some of the world's greatest scoundrels.'

Sasha found that easy to believe. They weren't all dead, either. One of them could very well be sitting opposite her. However, she adopted a professional air and spelled out *her* credentials for the job.

'I assure you, Mrs Wingate, it is quite straightforward. I've done this many times before. Civil registration was introduced into New South Wales in 1856. From that time onwards, there's been a legal and compulsory requirement for all births, deaths and marriages to be registered. Before that, there are baptismal and marriage and funeral entries in church registers. I can obtain these...'

'Is bigamy against the law?' Hester archly demanded.

'Yes.'

'That's what I thought.' She gave Sasha a knowing look. 'I wouldn't rely on every member of this family's observing the law all the time. Not when it comes to bigamy. And not in other matters either.'

Sasha flashed a simmering look at Nathan Parnell. He was certainly of a similar breed.

He gave her a wicked grin that confirmed he took an unholy joy in doing things *his* way. It also confirmed he was thoroughly enjoying this little contretemps between her and Hester Wingate.

'And this is only the beginning, my dear,' Hester went on. 'Many peculiar things happened in my family. I want answers to every question.'

Sasha wanted a few answers, too. 'I'll need to get as much of the background as you can give me, Mrs Wingate.'

The aforementioned Jane arrived with a traymobile loaded with refreshments. Either Hester Wingate had a good appetite or she expected Nathan and Sasha to eat plates of sandwiches, cakes, scones, and pastries.

'Now tell me, my dear,' Hester commanded, eyeing Sasha with challenging interest. 'How much do you charge for your services?'

Sasha was more than ready for that question. Since eccentricity was the order of the day, she was not to be outdone. 'Fifteen guineas an hour,' she said, rolling it out as though it was her standard fee and not to be blinked at. It translated to thirty-one dollars, fifty cents, which gave her a nice little bonus for heartburn.

'Oh, yes!' Hester cried in delight, turning a beaming smile to Nathan. 'She *is* clever!'

'There are two other conditions,' Sasha added. 'I'm only to be spoken of in the most commendable manner. And the money is to be paid on Fridays between the hours of nine a.m. and noon.'

If some devious game was being played, Sasha had decided she could play it with the best of them.

Hester Wingate leaned back in her chair, the enquiring blue eyes looking even more quizzical. 'How *very* clever of you! And perceptive.'

Uh-oh, Sasha thought. Had she gone too far? 'I hope I wasn't being impertinent,' she said in a swift attempt to mend fences. After all the job, bogus or not, did offer an easy and much needed income.

'Not at all,' Hester assured her. 'You've struck on the one person I want you to concentrate on most of all. Every bit of dirt you can find. He is the greatest rogue and villain that ever lived. He destroyed my life.

To get revenge on him when I meet him on the other side...my dear, I would pay you anything.'

'And that person is...?' Sasha prompted.

Hester frowned. 'I thought you already knew.'

'I'm not sure,' Sasha replied with a sinking feeling. Was she reading this situation wrongly?

'Why, my dear, the man in question is your benefactor.'

Sasha looked towards Nathan Parnell, desperately hoping she misunderstood. Despite his highly individual personality, and very wrong ideas about marriage, she wanted Nathan Parnell to be a *good* man, not a villain.

'Seagrave Dunworthy,' Hester said with hatred in her voice. 'The man I want to malign and crush is Seagrave Dunworthy.'

Sasha was stunned, all her assumptions shattered in one blow. There could be no doubting the depth of feeling emanating from Hester Wingate. Seagrave Dunworthy had been a real person. His eccentric will must be real as well. Hester Wingate's dirt-digging venture was real. The prospect of full employment for a long time to come was real. She had been told the truth.

Her eyes flew to Nathan Parnell. He *was* a good man. He had rescued her from Tyler, directed her to accommodation that met all her needs and more, directed her to a job that would help set her on her feet financially. He was better than Santa Claus.

Except there were two catches to the gifts he bestowed. The kind of marriage he wanted was anathema to her. And Sasha was now faced with a first-class dilemma.

If she did the job Hester Wingate required, and dug up dirt on Seagrave Dunworthy, she risked losing her low-rent accommodation at Seagrave Dunworthy's house. It was impossible to sustain a pose of highly esteeming a man if she proved he was a rogue and a villain.

The answer came to her. Nathan would know a way around the problem. He had got her into this mess. Now he had to get her out of it. And Sasha would make sure he did.

She smiled at him.

He smiled back at her.

Sasha's heart did a weird little flip.

How could she feel this sense of togetherness with a man she barely knew, a man who had no belief in the lasting power of love?

CHAPTER SIX

SASHA was shown the history room. Arrangements were made for her to examine all the contents the following day. Hester said Brooks, her chauffeur, would collect Sasha from Mosman and drive her home again. Nathan suggested that Hester acquire a photocopier. Hester told him to organise the purchase and delivery. She wasn't interested in mechanical things. That was what men were for.

How different it would be if it were a horse, Sasha thought, surprising herself with how readily she was accepting what would have been an alien world to her a week ago. But she couldn't allow herself to be swept too far from her own objectives. There were problems to be resolved, and the sooner she did it, the better.

She waited until they took their leave of Hester and were in the car again with Bonnie settled in the back seat. 'What did Seagrave Dunworthy do with his life?' she asked, wondering if Nathan Parnell was prepared to malign their benefactor.

'I never knew him personally. He died around the time of the First World War.'

Sasha had the feeling it was an evasive answer. 'Do you have a copy of his will?'

'No.'

'Well, I'll soon get one. And since this job was your brilliant idea, and you do have legal expertise with wills, you can tell me how I can satisfy Hester without breaking the "highly esteemed" clause.'

'Easy.' He grinned at her. 'Dig up the dirt Hester requires, then prove it's all wrong. A vicious attack by vicious people on a highly esteemed and worthy man.'

'Thank you. I knew you'd have an answer,' Sasha said drily, thinking Nathan had better be proved right on this important point.

He chuckled. 'You have quite a talent for answers yourself. You handle Hester very well.'

She was amused by his admiration for her stand on giving as good as she got. Although initially she had been completely thrown. 'There was a moment when I thought she might go so far as to check my muscle tone and sprinting ability.'

'Your muscle tone is great.' His voice throbbed with appreciation.

Sasha's amusement died. Had last night's embrace been a coldly calculated way of checking out her body? 'If you've been summing me up for *breeding* potential...'

He grinned at her look of outrage. 'Making babies wasn't on my mind when I had you in my arms.' The teasing twinkle melted into something much more direct. 'Making love was.'

A flood of heat suffused Sasha's body. She knew he was merely stating the truth, and she couldn't deny she had been tempted, but it was time to spell out her position. Unequivocally.

'That wasn't love. It was passion. And it will not suffice.'

'Pretty powerful stuff, all the same.' He raised his eyebrows at her. 'Are you saying you don't want to sample the experience again?'

She struggled between honesty and caution. His eyes wouldn't let her lie. 'No. But...'

'Encouraging.'

'...I want more than that,' she finished emphatically.

'You'll get it,' he said with relish.

'No. I meant it's not enough.'

'I can do better.'

'I'm not talking about sex, Nathan,' she cried in exasperation. 'I'm talking about... about sharing... and caring.'

'Good manners. That's what you're talking about. If you'd like to tell me what gives you the most pleasure...'

'Forget it.' So much for a sense of togetherness, Sasha berated herself. She and Nathan Parnell were on a totally different wavelength when it came to love. 'It's too soon after Tyler,' she argued. 'I hardly know you. I don't know that I want to know you. You could turn out to be as great a villain as Seagrave Dunworthy.'

Sasha gasped in horror at what she had said. She had just lost her accommodation for Bonnie and herself.

Nathan Parnell broke the strangling silence, his voice pitched low, but certainty behind every word, a seriousness she had never heard before, except for one occasion. 'When needs must,' he said. 'We all have to do things we'd rather not. What do you know, really know, about Seagrave Dunworthy, apart from titbits of gossip? Who knows anyone? I could have sworn I knew my ex-wife. I bet you thought you knew Tyler. We were both wrong.'

He was right about that, but Sasha couldn't bring herself to concede the point. She didn't want to open her mouth again after the awful blunder over her benefactor. She was intensely grateful to Nathan for excusing it.

She pondered the unpalatable truth of what he'd said. It was all too easy to be fooled by images, never really knowing what went on beneath the surface of a person. Maybe life was a lottery. Either good or bad luck ran with whom you drew as a partner.

On the other hand, she did have some freedom of choice in whom she selected and when she selected them. With Nathan Parnell, it was definitely too soon, and she would never accept *his* terms for marriage, no matter how attractive she found him.

She belatedly realised that Nathan had driven past the turn-off to the Mosman house. 'Where are you going?' she asked, her head swivelling around to check she was not mistaken.

'To the exhibition centre at Darling Harbour,' he answered matter-of-factly.

The diamonds!

Sasha relaxed. Her curiosity was piqued. It would surely reveal another facet of Nathan Parnell's extraordinary life.

It was a quick journey into the city. Nathan casually parked the car in a place reserved for VIPs at the exhibition centre. Sasha didn't say anything. Let him take the consequences when he was found out.

Bonnie had slept through the entire trip. The sound of the car doors being opened and closed woke her. Nathan elected to lift her out of the carrycot and carry her in his arms, insisting she was no burden at all. Bonnie made no protest at this arrangement, snuggling happily against his shoulder and cooing approval at Nathan.

Sasha was privately amazed at Bonnie's ready acceptance of him. Normally she cried if a stranger picked her up, especially a man. Even when Tyler had made an effort to appear fatherly, Bonnie had sensed his inner rejection of the role, exasperating Tyler with her non-co-operation in playing the adoring daughter.

Plainly it was different with Nathan. He looked perfectly comfortable with a baby perched in his arms. A big man but a tender one. A rock. A protector. Bonnie must sense that, Sasha decided. Maybe instincts were more trustworthy than any knowledge.

As they walked along together, she started wondering about Matt's mother. Didn't she miss him? Sasha couldn't understand a mother giving up her child unless forced to by painful circumstances, yet Nathan had implied that Matt's mother was like Tyler, hating the responsibilities of parenthood.

The hurt must have gone very deep when Nathan realised he'd made a mistake in his choice of wife. Clearly he did not want to subject himself to that kind of hurt again. But Sasha was sure it was a worse mistake to give up on love altogether. A marriage of convenience was not the answer.

On entering the main hall at the exhibition centre, Sasha very quickly realised diamonds were not the dominant feature on show. There were huge displays on all the mining ventures: models and maps and diagrams and videos of gold mining at Kalgoorlie; iron mining at Pilbura; copper mining at Mount Isa; silver-lead-zinc mining at Broken Hill; coal mining from the Newcastle region; opal mining at Cooper Pedy; and, of course, diamond mining in the Kimberleys, as well as many others.

School groups were being led around by teachers who were intent on broadening the education of their pupils. There were crowds of other people, as well, satisfying their interest in the natural resources of a country that was rich with minerals and precious stones.

'If you don't want a geology lesson, we'll go straight to the showroom,' Nathan said, refocusing Sasha's attention on why he had brought her here.

'Lead the way,' she replied, realising they didn't have unlimited time. Matt would have to be picked up from his playschool at some reasonable hour.

Two security guards stood on either side of the doorway into the showroom. Sasha was amazed there weren't more in evidence when she saw what was displayed with such little protection. There were signs saying no touching was allowed, and people were not to stray in any way beyond the roped off areas, but the nuggets and precious stones were not in locked glass cases. They were arrayed on velvet-covered stands, their full glory undiminished by any barriers to the naked eye.

The coloured diamonds were the centrepiece in the room. They *were* fabulous. Sasha had only seen white diamonds before. She was fascinated by the range and brilliance of the colours. They were worth a king's ransom. The most outstanding was a pink.

'Gorgeous, isn't it?' Nathan murmured.

'Magnificent,' she agreed.

'It really doesn't catch the light to best advantage on that velvet,' he suggested.

'The notice said no touching,' she warned, catching the drift of his intent.

'You're right,' he agreed. 'Let's take the diamond home and study it there.'

With a nonchalant air, he placed one leg across the roped off area. Nothing happened. Then, to Sasha's dazed disbelief, he reached out and palmed the diamond from its stand.

Her shocked eyes followed the movement.

Just as swiftly, the diamond was secreted inside Bonnie's pilchers, hidden in the folds of her nappy. Maintaining every appearance of total innocence, Nathan Parnell calmly stepped back into the visitors' area and turned to view the opals on the other side of the diamond display.

All hell broke loose.

Alarms soared up a scale of decibels. Klaxons whooped. Bonnie started wailing. The two security guards filled the doorway, ordering those in the showroom to stay precisely where they were. Excited yelling was accompanied by a stampede of running feet from the hall outside.

Sasha froze. Nathan Parnell was a jewel thief? He was using *her* baby as an accomplice in a diamond heist? Could he possibly think she would let him get away with it? Did he possibly think *he* could get away with it?

No wonder he had disagreements with judges about what constituted justice! He had handed her a lot of surprises but this was beyond the pale. No way would she involve herself with a thief!

The guards parted to allow more men into the room. The sirens stopped. The klaxons stopped. After all the noise the silence was startling. The first man pointed an accusing finger straight at Nathan. 'I've got you,' he said with absolute conviction. 'You put the diamond in the baby's nappy.'

Sasha felt a surge of relief. At least she didn't have to accuse him herself. But was she incriminated by being with him? Would anyone believe she wasn't an accessory in these circumstances?

'You made the baby cry,' Nathan admonished, making a great show of trying to soothe Bonnie.

Sasha was dumbfounded by his calm and cool demeanour. How could he remain so unaffected in the face of being caught red-handed?

An older man pushed forward. He glared long and hard at Nathan Parnell through his gold-rimmed spectacles, brushed a hand over his receding hairline, then with an air of dull resignation he said, 'All right, Mr Parnell. You've proved your point.'

'Did you get a good shot of me on video, Daniel?' Nathan drawled, tilting his chin this way and that in mock posturing. 'Did I show up well from every angle? Which profile gave the best result?'

Sasha shook her head in bewilderment. He sounded like a horribly vain movie star wanting his ego stroked.

Daniel's gloom appeared to deepen substantially. 'Mr Parnell, you photograph brilliantly from any angle. I really prefer not to choose a specific shot. But I ask you...I beg you...is it possible for you to visit the display and *not* set off the alarms, and *not* have your photograph taken?'

'Daniel, if I recollect perfectly...' his voice dripped with silky reasonableness '...harsh words were spoken...'

'Mr Parnell, no man regrets, genuinely regrets, as much as I do that I called you crazy.' Daniel's voice gathered a passionate momentum as he continued. 'No man can more sincerely believe that I made a great error of judgement when I said this protection system could not work. No man could have been more wrong when I said, if this system could work, you were the last person in the world capable of making it happen. No person could be more sincerely, genuinely regretful of past mistakes, and I beg you, I beseech you, I pray that you will take this admission as an act of contrition, a true humbling of self.'

Daniel took a deep breath. There was a pitiful crack in his voice as he confessed, 'You are making my life hell, Mr Parnell. Please...please...will you stop setting off the alarms?'

'The system works, Daniel,' came the stern reproof.

'It does indeed, Mr Parnell,' he agreed effusively.

'You're absolutely convinced of that, Daniel?'

'I shall laud this system, and your genius in making it work, to the four corners of the earth, Mr Parnell.'

Nathan sighed. 'Well, if you're prepared to guarantee it that far, I'll stop testing it.'

'Thank you, Mr Parnell. Thank you. Thank you.'

'You can now have your diamond back, Daniel,' he said, as though bestowing a great favour. He extracted it from Bonnie's nappy and started polishing it on his lapel.

'Kind of you, Mr Parnell. Very kind.'

'And I won't set the alarms off again. Or have my photos taken.'

'Mr Parnell, I'll mention you as a beneficiary in my will. Thank you.'

Nathan held out the diamond and Daniel gratefully accepted it. With great care and precision, he positioned it on its stand, then stepped away with the air of a man who'd had a great burden lifted from his shoulders.

'Computer games,' Sasha muttered, intensely relieved that it was a case of Nathan Parnell nailing someone rather than being nailed himself. He might be a rogue but he wasn't a villain.

Nathan grinned at her. 'I like practical results, even from games.'

'It works. It all works,' Daniel repeated with fervour, then made a hasty withdrawal.

'Seen enough?' Nathan asked Sasha.

'Yes, thank you.'

'Sorry about upsetting Bonnie. I didn't think of that.'

'You didn't think of my heart, either.'

'Maybe I did.' His eyes danced with unholy mischief. 'You don't have any hankering to lead an exciting life?'

'Not so I've noticed,' she replied drily.

'Don't worry about it. A little more exposure, a little more training, and you'll soon be doing things you never thought possible.'

'That is highly unlikely.'

'We'll see,' Nathan said blithely.

They made their exit from the exhibition centre, thankfully leaving behind the speculative interest of onlookers. Sasha breathed in the sweet air of freedom, released from the prospect of visiting Nathan Parnell in Long Bay Gaol. Whether it was sheer relief or Nathan's outrageous behaviour she didn't know, but she broke into laughter at the whole crazy incident as they walked towards the car park.

'What do you find so funny?' he asked.

He didn't look at all amused. Perhaps he thought she was laughing at his idea that more exposure to his way of living would immure her to anything happening.

'It just feels good to be alive,' she answered. He certainly put some new zest and zing into her life. In fact, she couldn't remember ever having had such a wildly eventful day. Maybe Nathan was right. Not only had she sustained a number of shocks, she seemed to be thriving on them.

She grinned at him. 'Next time you decide to walk into such a prestigious place and play a game with one of your toys, you could give me a hint that pandemonium is about to break out.'

'Hey, wait a bit,' he cautioned. 'That wasn't a game and it wasn't a toy.'

'Well, you found it amusing enough when you were doing it. I find it more amusing now.'

'That was very serious business,' he insisted.

'Getting your photo taken,' she mocked. 'Ringing all the bells. Driving that poor man to distraction.'

It didn't get the kind of response Sasha had grown used to from him. The eyes that bored into hers had no twinkle. His face suddenly looked older; grave, hard, bitten with a determination to survive any odds.

'If that *poor* man hadn't said what he did to me, I wouldn't have gone to the US to develop my system. If I hadn't gone to the US, I wouldn't have kept custody of Matt. If I hadn't been contracted to prove my system at the exhibition, I wouldn't have had to come back to Australia. Because I came back into the country, and got found out, I've got a custody case to fight...' for the first time he sounded and looked like a man under great stress and strain '...and the inevitable consequences.'

'Is there anything I can do to help?' The impulse to give whatever sympathetic comfort she could was instinctive.

Nathan Parnell looked at her, a fierce blaze of emotion making his eyes even more vividly blue. There was no surface amiability or pleasantness now. Sasha wondered if she could ever know the inner core of this man, if any one person could ever really understand another.

'I've run out of time,' he grated. 'I need a wife.'

CHAPTER SEVEN

SASHA felt her heart being squeezed. The force of his emotion was frightening and hurtful in its striking power. Sasha had never experienced anything like it. The urge to take it upon herself to solve his problems was compelling.

It took all her concentrated willpower to resist it, to turn her head away, keep walking. She was acutely conscious of him walking beside her, carrying Bonnie, a man who loved his son as she loved her daughter.

She didn't need to ask why a wife was so necessary to him. He had said enough for her to put two and two together. It was clearly related to keeping custody of his child. She felt sorry for him, deeply sorry that he was faced with the possibility of being parted from Matt. His love for the little boy had tugged at Sasha's heart from the moment of meeting in the park.

Nathan Parnell touched her in a way no man, or any human, had ever touched her, but she couldn't be his wife. Not as a convenience. His need to be married had nothing to do with her, not as the person she was. Sexual attraction was no basis for marriage. Neither was compassion. Sasha wanted to be loved, to be the only woman her husband would ever want beside him because no other woman would ever mean as much.

Tears pricked at her eyes. It wasn't fair that she should feel so drawn to a man who only wanted to marry her to secure his son from his ex-wife. And what about Matt's mother? Nathan had taken their son out of the country to keep custody, possibly bypassing the law, taking it into his own hands to do what he considered right. Maybe the woman had been grieving for her child. Sasha had only heard Nathan's view of his first marriage. How could she judge what was right and wrong?

They reached the car. Sasha remembered what she had thought about Nathan parking in a place reserved for VIPs. She hadn't known he was entitled to do so. It reinforced how little she knew about his life, what drove him to be the man he was. In the same way, he knew next to nothing about her. The idea of a marriage between them was dangerous. She had to stop thinking about it.

It was worse when they got in the car. Sasha was even more aware of him and it wasn't simply physical awareness. She felt pain and purpose pulsing in the silence. She desperately searched her mind for a way to break away from it, to separate herself from his need.

'So, you're now in the security business,' she said. His job was the only diversion she could come up with.

'More or less,' he answered, his tone uninterested, his thoughts clearly focused elsewhere.

'Would you mind explaining to me how your computer game works?' Sasha persisted.

There was little enthusiasm in his voice at first. Sasha suspected it was only good manners prompting his replies, but he gradually warmed to the subject under her skilful questioning.

She found out that touching the objects under protection did not set off the alarms. The public were deceived about this so they didn't put their fingerprints on things. The system worked on the principle of what Nathan called a violation of space.

Apparently this was very important to Nathan. He expounded on the theme on their way back to Mosman. The violation of space was measured or triggered—Sasha wasn't quite sure which—by comparing digitalised information from different sources—whatever that meant.

The whole concept sounded ingeniously clever. Any kind of normal movement close to the protected objects was discounted. It was the opposite of a video security system that sought to capture every piece of information, over ninety-nine per cent of which was wasted. This system excluded irrelevant information, only reacting to a very specific computation.

It was all a bit too technical for Sasha to fully comprehend but she listened intently because Nathan was clearly proud of his work, and from the sound of it he had every right to be.

They were close to home when Nathan turned the car off the main route. 'We're back earlier than I expected,' he said, 'so I'll pick Matt up and save Marion the trouble of doing it later on.'

They stopped at a pre-school kindergarten centre. Nathan was able to park right outside the gate. 'This can take up to ten minutes or so, Sasha,' he warned. 'Do you want to come with me?'

'I'll wait here if you don't mind.' She needed the relief from keeping up a friendly interest and trying to ignore what was none of her business.

He had no sooner left her than Bonnie awoke. The motion of a car always put her to sleep, but once it stopped there were invariably cries of protest. Sasha decided a little distraction was in order. The kindergarten playground was swarming with small children taking part in one activity or another. Sasha lifted Bonnie out of the car and strolled over to the wire fence, knowing her baby daughter would soon be fascinated by the novelty of watching other children at play.

'Bonnie!' An excited cry pealed across the playground. A group of boys broke apart as one of them raced towards the fence. 'Bonnie, it's me, Matt!'

It was, indeed, and Bonnie responded as though she remembered him, waving her arms and gurgling with pleasure.

'Did Daddy bring you?' he asked Sasha, his face wreathed in a happy smile, his blue eyes dancing with delight.

'Yes.' Sasha nodded to the building. 'He's gone inside to collect you.'

'I'm out here,' Matt said unnecessarily. He turned to his friends who had followed him over. 'See? I have got a baby to play with,' he said triumphantly. 'She's a little girl, and my Daddy said I could help look after her 'cause she's living in our house now.'

'Boys are more fun than girls,' one boy observed.

'I like girls,' Matt said very seriously.

Sasha couldn't help smiling.

One of the other boys eyed her up and down. 'Are you Matt's mother?'

'Course she is!' Matt insisted, wheeling on the doubter. 'I told you she was coming.'

Sasha, who had opened her mouth to deny it, promptly held her tongue. She remembered the taunting in her own childhood about the lack of a father. No one believed she had one because he was mostly away in the navy. She had always felt the odd person out. What harm was there in letting Matt win at least one round with his playmates?

She would have to correct him once they were alone together. She could not allow him to continue the fiction. But for the present, it didn't matter much at all. In fact, it was quite flattering to be accepted so readily. Perhaps it reflected the little boy's deep inner yearning for a mother.

'Are you going to live with Matt now?' another boy asked, checking out the facts.

'Yes,' Sasha answered. 'Bonnie and I have come to stay.'

Matt beamed his pleasure in her affirmation. 'I can show Bonnie lots of things,' he said, his eyes shining at the prospect of having a ready admirer at hand from now on.

'Matt! Your father's here,' a woman called, beckoning him into the school building.

Matt sped off like a frisky colt, running and leaping for joy that his world was set to rights, at least for one day. The other boys trailed away from the fence, and Sasha returned to the car.

A minute or two later, Nathan and Matt appeared, the little boy swinging on his father's hand, skipping along beside him, obviously cock-a-hoop about having a 'family'.

Matt was strapped into his car seat beside Bonnie. As Nathan drove them home, the little boy excitedly told Bonnie of his favourite toys and what they could do with them. Bonnie made approving noises.

'I'll drop you at the front door before I garage the car, Sasha,' Nathan said as he turned the BMW into the driveway. 'If you'd like to leave the carrycot and simply lift Bonnie out, I'll carry it up for you later.'

'Can I get out with Bonnie, Daddy?' Matt asked.

'We'd better go and see Marion first, Matt. If it's all right with Sasha, you can then visit Bonnie.'

Sasha turned to give the little boy a welcoming smile. 'Whenever you're ready, Matt.'

'It'll be real soon,' he replied eagerly.

The car stopped at the front steps and Sasha quickly assured Nathan she didn't need him to get out and help. She collected her holdall, picked up Bonnie, thanked Nathan for everything, and closed the car doors on father and son.

As she unlocked the front door and entered the house, Sasha wished she could enjoy a sense of homecoming. The events of the day had left her with very mixed feelings about how to handle living here with Nathan Parnell and his son. Last night it had seemed relatively clear-cut. Even this morning she had thought all the choices were hers to make. Which they were. But they didn't feel quite so clear-cut any more.

Her arms full with carrying Bonnie and her bag, Sasha pushed the front door closed with her shoulder, then noticed that the double doors from the lounge to the foyer were wide open. Marion must be doing some cleaning, Sasha thought, and looked in to say hello to the housekeeper.

There was a woman in the room but it wasn't Marion Bennet. Nor could she be remotely connected to cleaning. She had made herself comfortable in one of the armchairs, a drink in one hand, a smouldering cigarette in the other, and she had the look of being perfectly at home, having been born and bred to a rich and luxurious setting.

On catching sight of Sasha, she raised a finely arched eyebrow that somehow projected both curiosity and condescension. 'Who have we here?' she asked in a tone that simulated interest but had absolutely no heart in it.

Sasha did not reply. Her mind was busy trying to place the face which was elusively familiar to her. The woman crushed her cigarette into an ashtray and stood up. She wasn't beautiful. She was elegant. She was class from head to toe.

Blonde hair was tucked into a smooth French pleat but an artful fringe added a soft dash of femininity. Her make-up made the most of an interesting and very individual bone-structure. She was tall and excessively slim. The tailored cream suit she wore was pinstriped with navy. Pearls made the perfect accessory.

She strolled towards Sasha, one hand still nursing her drink, a smile playing on her rather thin lips, a superior smile, not one with any warmth in it.

'I'm Nathan Parnell's wife,' she said. 'Who are you?'

CHAPTER EIGHT

BIGAMY leapt into Sasha's mind. The bottom fell out
of her world. Nathan Parnell hit the lowest rung of the
ladder, and was shelved in the darkest, deepest recess
in the basement.

Yet . . . he had been good to her. And kind. She
forced out the necessary words with the necessary
aplomb. 'I thought *ex-wife* was the situation.'

The woman shrugged. 'Life is change. Change is
life. Discords can be turned into melodies. Who can
say?' Again the smile without warmth, an automatic
mechanism that declared she was in control of herself
and everything else.

But she *was* the ex-wife. Sasha was satisfied that
Nathan Parnell had not lied. His position zoomed out
of the basement cellar and returned to the top of the
ladder. She might not want to marry Nathan Parnell
herself, but she certainly didn't want any other woman
getting him before she made up her mind. Whether it
was his ex-wife or not simply didn't matter. Not to
Sasha.

'Don't count on a melody,' she said, wanting to
shake the woman's insufferable confidence.

'Oh?' The eyebrow lifted in supercilious amusement. 'You're in a position to judge, are you?'

'I live here.'

The woman's calculating grey eyes flicked to Bonnie, studied her for a moment, then dismissed the baby as of no account. She added a curl of condescension to her smile. 'Nathan always was a sucker for down-and-outs.'

It ripped the mat out from under Sasha's feet momentarily, but she came back fighting. 'That's to my advantage, don't you think?'

'Dream on.'

The derisive reply was cuttingly dismissive. Sasha struggled for a suitable riposte.

'Elizabeth!'

The whip-like command in the call of the name snapped the friction between the two women. They turned to look at its source. Nathan Parnell had entered the lounge by the door from the hall. He did not look at all pleased to see his visitor.

'Yes, darling. I've come back,' Elizabeth drawled in a sacharine sweet voice.

'What for?'

No warmth there. Good, Sasha thought. No move to greet his ex-wife in any welcoming way, either. He stood by the door, grim-faced, his eyes ablaze with bitter suspicion.

Elizabeth strolled away from Sasha, but not towards her ex-husband. She stopped in front of the fireplace, as though establishing her hold on a commanding position. The three of them now formed a triangle, all equally separated. Sasha began to realise how formidable this woman was.

'You need a wife, Nathan,' Elizabeth stated without preamble. 'I'm qualified for the job. More experience than any other woman. I'll even forgive you your indiscretion.' She glanced at Sasha as though she were a *mycobacterium leprae bacillus.*

Nathan said nothing. His gaze did not shift from his ex-wife. Sasha suddenly felt very much out of place, an interloper in highly private business.

'If you'll excuse me . . .'

'No.' Nathan's attention snapped to her, the blue eyes compelling in their intensity of feeling. 'Please stay. I want you to hear.'

'You're always so cautious and conservative, Nathan,' Elizabeth mocked.

'If you're sure,' Sasha said uncertainly.

'He wants you as a witness, you fool! Not that it will do him any good.'

The scorn stung. Sasha looked at Nathan's supremely superior ex-wife and felt a slow, deep anger start to burn. Tyler, in his worst moments, used to call her a fool. He implied all women were fools, driven by their hormones. Here was a woman calling her a fool, and Sasha wasn't about to take it, not from anyone.

'I'll bet she doesn't have any hormones,' she gritted between gnashing teeth.

'Too damned right,' Nathan agreed. 'Perceptive of you. No hormones.'

The woman viewed Sasha with icy contempt. 'Beware of slander. I have a law degree, the same as Nathan.'

Dismissing Sasha as too trivial for further consideration, she turned back to the target of her visit. 'We have a custodial case on our hands, Nathan. I came to give you a choice. You can remarry me and play the part of the adoring husband, which you do so well, for the next twelve years. In that time I will become the first female premier of this state and have two terms in office.'

Enlightenment burst through Sasha's mind. The vague familiarity of the face—Elizabeth Maddox— prominent campaigner on television in the last state election—the consummate speaker for *women's* interests.

'That satisfies my needs,' she continued, uncaring of the naked and grasping ambition she displayed. 'You get to keep Matt, Nathan. That will satisfy your needs.'

'If *needs must*.' It was the voice of hopelessness.

Sasha was appalled at the deal offered and Nathan's response to it. 'That is so unfair!' The words poured from her lips before she could bite her tongue. 'It's blackmail!'

The woman shrugged. It was of no consequence to her whether it was fair or not. Sasha's heart plummeted to the same basement dungeon where she had previously put Nathan Parnell. She looked at him in desperate appeal. Was there no way out of this poisonous woman's plot?

He misread her look. 'Elizabeth didn't become avaricious for power over people until after we married,' he said, as though wanting Sasha to understand there was some mitigation for his mistake in marrying the woman.

'It took me a while to realise my potential,' Elizabeth agreed. 'But I made it big. And I'm going to make it bigger. One day I'm going to be the first female prime minister of this country. My name will be enshrined in every history book.'

The gloating pride in her voice sent a wave of revulsion through Sasha. The self-aggrandisement was sickening enough, but then she had the gall to look at Nathan as though he were an object of pity.

'And what will you have done, Nathan? What will you achieve?' she mocked.

He made no reply, simply staring stonily at his ex-wife. And Sasha suddenly understood. There was no point in talking caring or kindness or generosity of heart to a heart of stone. Nor would Elizabeth give credit to any genius of mind that was not bent to amassing and cementing power.

'I'll expose you,' Sasha said, fiercely hating everything Elizabeth Maddox stood for. 'I'll repeat this conversation. As a witness. I'll sell it to the newspapers. I'll...'

Elizabeth laughed at her. 'You'd be digging yourself a hole you'd never climb out of, you poor, pathetic idiot. You couldn't pay off the damages I'd collect in a lifetime.'

'I could show up your rotten hypocrisy so you'd never get elected again,' Sasha flung back at her.

'No one would believe you by the time I finished ripping your character to shreds,' she retorted with chilling confidence. 'In the courtroom I can make black look white and white look black.'

She looked pointedly at Bonnie, then eyed Sasha with malicious intent. 'I think I'd portray you as a…tramp. A gold-digger. A sleazy gutter bitch who's trying to sell something more profitable than what's between her legs. I can do it, too, can't I, Nathan?'

'Yes,' he agreed heavily. 'You can do it, Elizabeth.'

She didn't bother acknowledging the affirmation. Her cold reptilian eyes kept projecting their lethal message straight at Sasha. 'That was the difference between us. Nathan was an idealist. He wanted truth and justice, no matter at what cost. I wanted success. I won. Nathan lost. That's true, isn't it, Nathan?'

'Yes,' he agreed even more heavily. 'You won. I lost.'

It answered all the questions Sasha had had about why Nathan was no longer a barrister. And why he took the law into his own hands to correct what he perceived as wrong.

Elizabeth bestowed her smarmy smile on him. 'That's the way it's always been between us. You recognise and accept that, don't you, Nathan?'

'I hope you never make yourself Minister for Justice,' he said, hating his defeat yet apparently powerless to evade it.

'Why would you lose the custody case?' Sasha pleaded to him. 'If the family law court has already found in your favour…'

'Please explain it to your moronic friend, Nathan.'

He took a deep breath. He looked directly into Sasha's eyes, yet his own were curiously blank. There was nothing to be read of what he was feeling. His voice was toneless as he stated the position.

'The reality was that Matt would have interfered with Elizabeth's working schedule. I interfered with it and she got rid of me. The responsibility of a child was a worse interference so she got rid of Matt. At the time, that image of Elizabeth and her ambition suited her requirements. My petition to the court for custody was not contested. It suited Elizabeth to let me have Matt then. But when it comes to court again, she will argue mental fatigue and harassment, undue pressure by a big powerful man on a defenceless woman. Allegations will be made of physical threats . . . is that right, Elizabeth?'

'It barely scrapes the surface of what will happen, Nathan,' came the taunting promise.

'Now that Elizabeth has her eye on high office, she has to project family values, loyalties, caring and concern for people.' A touch of acid crept into his voice at associating such things with a woman to whom they meant nothing. 'What was good for her ambition before is now a liability. Voters want to see personal warmth. Matt is to be her showpiece . . .'

'And you, darling,' Elizabeth drawled. 'Devoted husband and father. I want both Matt and you to give my new image solid credibility.'

His jaw tightened. It clearly took an effort to unclench his teeth and continue. 'It will be argued in court that I prevented Elizabeth from knowing her own son because I went to the US which prevented her exercising visiting rights.'

Sasha couldn't let that pass. 'But you went to the US because Daniel rejected your system and . . .'

'We're not talking about truth, Sasha,' Nathan cut in, a thread of passion breaking through the mono-tone. 'We're talking what will be argued.'

'You've learnt a lot in the last year or so, Nathan,' Elizabeth remarked, then enjoyed herself by driving a few more nails into the argument. 'Alienation of nat-ural love and affection ... I'll have a field day in the Press. Women everywhere will naturally sympathise with my plight against this bullying man.'

It was a total travesty of justice and she relished it, Sasha thought, feeling both helpless and hopeless in the face of such consciousless and callous manipula-tion of others' lives.

Nathan didn't bother explaining any further. The situation was explicit enough. He was up against a ruthless woman who didn't care what damage she did as long as she won her own way.

Seeing that she was not about to draw more blood from Nathan, Elizabeth shrugged carelessly and said, 'Where is the child anyway? I suppose I should see him.'

If looks could kill, Nathan Parnell's look would have killed Elizabeth right there. She should have gone to hell and perdition, Sasha thought.

'If you want me to fall in with your scheme, Eliza-beth, you damned well put on your best political act with Matt.'

'Mummy awaits,' she syruped back at him.

He glowered disgust at her and left the room.

Elizabeth finished her drink and set the glass on the mantelpiece. She turned to Sasha. 'I suppose you're paying some pittance rent under the will of Seagrave Dunworthy?'

Sasha disdained a reply. She wasn't going to feed this woman's malice.

Elizabeth sneered. 'What an old fool he was. Brain the size of a peanut. A walrus could have outperformed him in high intellectual capacity. And making such a clown of himself, at his age, with all that passion over such a contemptible girl, illegitimate child and all.'

Sasha held her tongue. She had no idea what Elizabeth was talking about and she wasn't about to show ignorance.

The other woman's gaze travelled around the room as though cataloguing its contents. 'Still, he did leave something of value and substance. Pity I'll never inherit, although, of course, under a tontine, anything is possible.'

A tontine! Sasha's mind did a swift whirl. Seagrave Dunworthy's will must be more eccentric than she'd thought. Under a tontine, the beneficiaries of an annuity shared in a trust, the shares increasing as each beneficiary died, until the whole went to the last survivor. Did this mean that Elizabeth Maddox was related to Seagrave Dunworthy? Or were Nathan and Matt?

The avaricious grey eyes returned to Sasha. 'Don't bet on staying here, rent or no rent. I'll make sure you'll very quickly lose any desire to remain under this roof.'

Nathan came back in, leading Matt by the hand. The little boy lagged a step behind, hesitant about

3 WAYS TO PLAY

see inside

for big CASH prizes and FREE GIFTS!

First play your "Win-A-Fortune" game tickets
to qualify for up to
<u>ONE MILLION DOLLARS IN LIFETIME INCOME</u>
– that's $33,333.33 each year for 30 years!

WIN A CASH F⦿RTUNE

GAME TIX NO.
1a

Game Ticket values vary. Scratch GOLD from Big Money
Wheel to determine the potential cash value of prize you will
receive if this ticket has a prizewinning sweepstakes number.

YOUR EXCLUSIVE
LUCKY NUMBER IS   2U339541

DO NOT SEPARATE—KEEP ALL GAMES INTACT

WIN A CASH F⦿RTUNE

GAME TIX NO.
1b

Game Ticket values vary. Scratch GOLD from Big Money
Wheel to determine the potential cash value of prize you will
receive if this ticket has a prizewinning sweepstakes number.

YOUR EXCLUSIVE
LUCKY NUMBER IS   1E120632

DO NOT SEPARATE—KEEP ALL GAMES INTACT

WIN A CASH F⦿RTUNE

GAME TIX NO.
1c

Game Ticket values vary. Scratch GOLD from Big Money
Wheel to determine the potential cash value of prize you will
receive if this ticket has a prizewinning sweepstakes number.

YOUR EXCLUSIVE
LUCKY NUMBER IS   5A134550

DO NOT SEPARATE—KEEP ALL GAMES INTACT

WIN A CASH F⦿RTUNE

GAME TIX NO.
1d

Game Ticket values vary. Scratch GOLD from Big Money
Wheel to determine the potential cash value of prize you will
receive if this ticket has a prizewinning sweepstakes number.

YOUR EXCLUSIVE
LUCKY NUMBER IS   7N323546

DO NOT SEPARATE—KEEP ALL GAMES INTACT

WIN A CASH F⦿RTUNE

GAME TIX NO.
1e

Game Ticket values vary. Scratch GOLD from Big Money
Wheel to determine the potential cash value of prize you will
receive if this ticket has a prizewinning sweepstakes number.

YOUR EXCLUSIVE
LUCKY NUMBER IS   9T463597

DO NOT SEPARATE—KEEP ALL GAMES INTACT

FOLD ALONG DOTTED LINE AND DETACH CAREFULLY

With a coin, carefully scratch off the three gold boxes. Then check the chart below to learn how many FREE BOOKS will be yours!

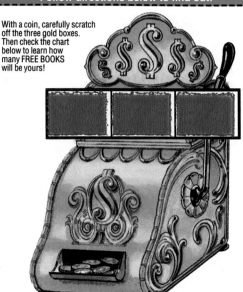

7	**7**	**7**	WORTH FOUR FREE BOOKS!
🔔	🔔	**BAR**	WORTH THREE FREE BOOKS!
🍒	🍒	**BAR**	WORTH TWO FREE BOOKS!
BAR	**BAR**	**BAR**	WORTH ONE FREE BOOK!

You'll receive brand-new Harlequin Presents® novels. When you scratch off the gold boxes and return this card in the reply envelope provided, we'll send you the books you qualify for <u>absolutely free</u>.

Harlequin
Reader Service®

Dear Reader,

Get out a coin—kiss it for good luck—and go to work on the WIN-A-FORTUNE tickets enclosed. You could end up a <u>million</u> <u>dollars</u> richer!

By returning these tickets you'll also be in the running for hundreds of other cash prizes we'll be giving away. It costs nothing to play this game—there's no fee, and no purchase is necessary!

We're holding this sweepstakes to introduce you to the benefits of the Harlequin Reader Service®. Scratch off the gold boxes on the enclosed Lucky 7 Slot Machine Game and we'll send you <u>free books</u>!

How many FREE BOOKS will you get? Play the Slot Machine Game and see! These books are absolutely free, with no obligation to buy anything!

The Harlequin Reader Service is **not** like some book clubs. We charge you nothing—ZERO—for your first shipment. And you don't have to make any minimum number of purchases—not even one!

over, please

FOLD ALONG DOTTED LINE AND DETACH CAREFULLY

For example, you could accept your FREE BOOKS and cancel immediately, by writing "please cancel" on the shipping statement and returning it to us. You'll owe nothing and be under no further obligation!

But the fact is, thousands of readers enjoy receiving books by mail from the Reader Service. They look forward to getting the best new romance novels months before they arrive in bookstores. And they like our discount prices!

I'm hoping that after receiving your free books you'll want to remain a subscriber. But the choice is yours—to continue or cancel, any time at all!

Pamela Powers

Pamela Powers for Harlequin

P.S. If you're accepting free books, play the "Ace of Hearts" game for a *free MYSTERY GIFT!*

what was expected of him. Nathan squatted down so that his eyes were on a level with his son's. He spoke softly but very seriously.

'Matt, I want you to meet someone very special to you. The most special person in the world. It's your Mummy, Matt.'

The little boy's gaze fixed on Elizabeth.

She gave her automatic smile. 'Hello, Matt.' It was the indulgent voice of a politician on an ingratiating mission, a concession to Nathan's demand. She held out her arms, inviting the child to run to her.

He did not. He sidled closer to his father and put his arms around Nathan's neck.

'Please, Matt,' Nathan gently begged. He tried to ease the stranglehold of Matt's arms, urging him into acceptance. 'Come with me and meet your...'

'She's my mother,' he whispered, flinging an arm out of Nathan's hold and pointing backwards at Sasha, but not looking at her. 'The same as Bonnie, Daddy.'

'No, Matt. You know we cannot tell a lie...'

'You said you were a police officer.'

Nathan winced. He was lost for words, for an adequate reply.

Sasha stepped in, trying to retrieve the situation. 'I'm your pretend mother, Matt. I love being your pretend mother, but Elizabeth is your real mother.'

'No, she's not,' Matt cried, and shook his head in adamant rejection.

Elizabeth's arms dropped to her sides. 'Let the boy go,' she said, and promptly cast aside any pretence of a maternal role. 'I merely wanted to see what he looks like. He takes after you, Nathan. Nothing of me there at all. What a pity. A fine-looking boy apart from that. He'll photograph well.'

Nathan struggled to his feet. 'Can't we try... ?'

'No. It's years before he becomes a voter,' Elizabeth said, as coldly practical as ever. 'Then he may comprehend my real worth.'

Again Nathan's jaw tightened, but he swiftly unlocked it to attend to his son. 'Do you want to go back to Marion, Matt?'

The boy fled the room without a backward glance. Nathan heaved a sigh and closed the door before turning to face Elizabeth again, his face etched in stoic resignation.

'Now let's get down to business,' Elizabeth said crisply. 'Do you want to marry me and keep the child, Nathan? Or do you want to lose a battle on the front page of the newspapers, as well as in the courtroom? What's your choice?'

When needs must, Sasha thought. The situation was very clear to her now. If Nathan Parnell was married to another woman, and they had a good, stable, old-fashioned, permanent relationship, the child's welfare would best be served, in the eyes of the court, by leaving custody as it was, with the father who could offer his son a secure family life. Visiting rights would go to Elizabeth, but Sasha had seen enough. The visiting rights would never be exercised.

'Come, Nathan, the decision does not call for deep reflection,' Elizabeth snapped impatiently. 'Make up your mind.'

His lips compressed. Sasha could feel his hatred of the decision facing him, yet, knowing his love for his son, she was also intensely aware of the sense of inevitability hanging over it.

Elizabeth, scenting victory, could not resist one more shaft. 'And you can throw this presumptuous hussy out of here today,' she said with a contemptuous toss of her hand at Sasha. 'I wish to occupy your bed tonight. See if you are still as expert as you once were.'

Manhood...fatherhood...she was taking him for everything. And Sasha knew Nathan would sacrifice it all to safeguard his son. The distaste on his face at this very moment would be swallowed. Whatever he had to do, no matter how dreadful it would be, he would do it for love of Matt. A rock. A protector.

His lips parted to form one word.

Sasha got in first. She did not recognise her own voice. It issued forth like the disembodied utterance of a spirit from another world.

'Mr Parnell does not have a choice.'

For the first time Elizabeth looked discomposed. She had been hanging on Nathan's word, already tasting her malicious triumphant success, knowing how he had been going to answer.

'Rubbish!' she hurled at Sasha, furious at the interruption. 'Everyone has choices.'

'Not in this case,' Sasha said with quiet determination. 'As a man of honour, Mr Parnell is already committed to a different future. He has asked me to marry him. And my answer...'

She felt him look at her. She looked at him and felt a wild sense of exultation as she saw the light of salvation in his eyes, the incredible reality of a miracle that he'd been given no reason to expect or hope for.

On a bursting wave of adrenaline, Sasha walked towards him. 'My absolute and unequivocal answer...' her voice gathered an evangelical passion '...is yes. I will marry him. Yes. And I'll stand by his side, in court and out of it, and fight his fights with him, against anyone and anything.'

She stopped in front of him and the admiration in his eyes was all the intoxicant she needed to drive the heady recklessness further. She wheeled to face their mutual enemy. 'You may not realise it yet, Elizabeth, but you're a loser. And you've just lost everything.'

'Nathan...' There was fury and frustration in the demand.

Sasha felt his arm curl around her shoulders, supporting her stand. 'I have a wife, Elizabeth,' he said, his voice strong and vibrant. 'So get the hell out of here. Sasha and I have matters of importance to discuss.'

CHAPTER NINE

SASHA had been so caught up with disposing of Nathan's ex-wife that she hadn't stopped to consider the consequences. They came to her hard and fast as Elizabeth Maddox made her final exit from Seagrave Dunworthy's home. At least, Sasha hoped it was the final exit.

She was beginning to realise what an incredibly reckless thing she'd done in committing herself to a marriage she didn't want. It could ruin her life. And Bonnie's. Nathan Parnell might be the sexiest man she had ever met, but however expert he was in bed, it wouldn't make up for a loveless relationship. On top of that, she would be trapped into staying with it by Matt, who wanted her to be his mother.

As the front door closed behind Elizabeth Maddox, the arm around Sasha's shoulders felt more like a prison bar than a source of comfort. 'I need to sit down, Nathan,' she said, but what she really needed was space and distance between them so she could start getting things in perspective.

Without a word he led her to one of the chesterfield lounges flanking the fireplace. She sank onto the soft down cushions and let Bonnie slide to her lap. The scene with Elizabeth had been harrowing and Sasha felt drained of initiative. Yet whatever she now said to Nathan Parnell was probably going to be the most important conversation of her life.

She groped for words and how to express them. She looked around the lounge, seeking inspiration. Such a beautiful room: chairs and sofas upholstered in silk brocades—peach, pale green, ivory and gold—their richness enhanced by a cream carpet that was both fine and thick. Elizabeth Maddox had fitted into this room. It was the appropriate gathering place for people of class to relax and enjoy each other's company Nathan Parnell looked right in it, too.

Sasha didn't fit at all. Not only was her bright lipstick pink dress a jarring tone, she simply wasn't used to an elegant lifestyle. It made her acutely conscious that she knew nothing of Nathan's friends, or the society in which he moved.

She wished he would sit down, preferably in the chesterfield opposite her, but apparently he wasn't going to. As though wanting to exorcise Elizabeth's image from this room, he stood where she had stood, in front of the fireplace. His hands were linked behind his back. He appeared to be studying the subtle peach shades around the veining in the marble top of the table set between the two sofas.

Sasha tried to read his face. What thoughts were running through his mind? There was no sign of joy or relief. No glance of gratitude to Sasha. No flash of wicked blue from his eyes. His demeanour was gravely introspective.

'Perhaps,' she began nervously, 'I acted somewhat hastily.'

In an instant his eyes were locked on to hers. 'You were *magnificent.*'

It took Sasha's breath away. No one had ever thought her that   nderful before. She was sorely tempted to bask b .he sweet intoxication of his admiration, but it was like the blissful afterglow of great sex. It wouldn't last.

'I shouldn't have let myself become involved,' she said, trying to get things on to a more practical level.

'Joan of Arc would have been proud of you.'

He was making it very, very difficult. 'There has to be another way out,' she said desperately.

'There is.'

Sasha looked at him incredulously. 'There is?'

The blue eyes bored into hers, intensely watchful. 'If you want it.'

'What do you mean, *if* I want it? You don't imagine I really want to marry you, do you?'

'It felt like a good idea to me.'

'That's because it's convenient,' she scoffed.

'You haven't felt a rather special feeling developing between us?'

Nathan Parnell had something up his sleeve. Probably an ace. Or a joker. Having seen him in action at the exhibition centre with the diamond, Sasha had little doubt it was a winning card. She could feel the confidence of the man and knew from hair-raising personal experience it would not be unfounded.

She had already entangled herself once. She was not going to do it again, not if there was a way out. She would treat Nathan Parnell with a great deal of circumspection, play her own cards very close to the chest, admit nothing. He was not going to get her more involved when she quite desperately needed to get herself uninvolved.

After her Joan of Arc triumph over Elizabeth, it was perfectly obvious that *feelings* could lead one badly astray. Sasha was not about to discuss such a dangerous and treacherous subject.

'I don't know what you mean,' she answered warily.

'Do you feel an animal magnetism between us?'

Sex, he meant, and that had to be trouble. 'Absolutely not,' she said primly.

'Do you feel a real need to be together for the sheer joy of being together?'

'I don't mind talking to you,' she conceded. That was relatively safe.

'A rapport that's beginning to be beautiful to share?'

She raised her eyebrows. 'When I don't know half the things I need to know about you?'

'Falling in love could have more to do with instinct than knowledge.'

'I've never heard anything more ridiculous in my life. How arrogant can you get, thinking I'm falling in love with you?'

He sighed and dropped his gaze, releasing Sasha from the disturbing directness that she had fended off with brick-wall effectiveness. She was congratulating herself on not letting down her guard when he shattered it with a sad personal reflection.

'Well, I guess the feeling is all on my side.'

Sasha's heart flipped around. Nathan Parnell, falling in love with her? That put a different complexion on things. Maybe she should stop giving blanket denials. If there was a real possibility... On the other hand, she had told him she wouldn't marry without love. This could be a ploy to win her over to the idea that a future together might be the answer to all her dreams, while its only real purpose was to solve his problems.

Would he be that low?

She scrutinised him as he studied the marble top again. He looked very sober and serious. If there weren't a determined jut to his chin, she might have said he looked depressed. After all, he had every reason to be depressed with the situation he faced with Elizabeth.

Sasha reconsidered. Maybe she should marry him. In name only, of course, just to get him over the hump of the legal situation. She wouldn't commit herself to a consummated marriage. There would have to be a way out. She could be a pretend wife and a pretend mother until the danger from Elizabeth was over. And then...

'Sasha...' He lifted pained eyes. A sharp touch of regret, a dull edge of resignation. 'There's been a grave misunderstanding. I don't quite know how to tell you this...'

Was it the truth? The unvarnished, unbent truth? Sasha had the impression of a great pit yawning open before her feet. Nathan was deadly serious and, whatever the misunderstanding was, it was going to affect her. Badly. She could feel it coming.

'Spell it out, Nathan,' she said, impatient to know the worst.

He hesitated. 'Let me get this absolutely clear. You really don't want to marry me?'

Sasha hesitated. Was she blocking off a door she really wanted left open? 'The circumstances are hardly propitious,' she said carefully, trying to keep all the options open.

'I can't help the circumstances, Sasha.'

'You did say there was another way,' she reminded him.

'You'd rather I take it?'

'That would certainly be best for me.' It gave her more time to explore what was happening between them, to make sure it was not a passing fancy.

'So what you said to Elizabeth was a ploy, a strategy, a tactic?'

'It was like you with Tyler in the park. Telling him you were a police officer to make him stop what he was doing to me.'

He nodded, closed his eyes briefly, then made a fair attempt at a grateful smile. 'I thank you, very sincerely, for standing up for me.'

'No one has the right to force their will on others. Elizabeth has no more right to do that than Tyler or anyone else.'

'I agree.' He nodded some more, took a deep breath, then added, 'And now that Elizabeth has been suitably diverted, I can get on with what really has to be done.'

Sasha frowned at him. 'What do you mean, Elizabeth was suitably diverted? I *saved* you from Elizabeth.'

'Yes, you did. I've never seen anything to equal it. Inspirational. I'll remember this day all my life.'

Sasha was somewhat mollified by the accolade but he hadn't answered her question. 'How will you beat her custody case if you don't marry me?'

'There is an alternative.'

'Yes?'

'When you were moving in yesterday, Matt and I went visiting. Marion told me you were short of work, so I interested Hester in your potential. But Matt and I did one other thing, as well.'

'What?'

'I signed a contract...establishing that...well, the long and short of it is that I've contracted another marriage arrangement.'

'You did *what?*' Sasha could scarcely believe her ears.

'She's a nice young Polish woman. Needs permanent residential status in this country. The problem was quite simple really. She wants...'

The wrath Sasha had felt against Elizabeth Maddox faded into insignificance. Two atoms collided. Nuclear fusion was about to take place.

'Nathan...' her voice shook with explosive energy '...do you realise that a few minutes ago I sacrificed myself, and Bonnie, and our future...we sacrificed ourselves for you? I went into battle for you, giving everything I had? I...'

'No one could more deeply appreciate...'

'And you are already contracted to marry another woman?'

'I had to do it.' He looked bewildered by her furious outburst. 'Time was running out. I told you so.'

Sasha hoisted Bonnie up to her shoulder again and rose to her feet. 'Precisely what did you have on your mind when you got me to come to this house, Nathan Parnell?'

'I didn't get you to come,' he protested. 'You needed a home...'

'You got me a job, as well.'

'So you'd have some income if you needed it.'

'And the very first night, after coming home from your Polish woman... Is she beautiful?'

'Well, yes, she is. I have to make the marriage look credible to Elizabeth, and...'

It was like waving a red rag at a bull. Sasha saw blood-red. 'So after coming home from your young, *beautiful* wife-to-be, you had the unspeakable duplicity to try your *passion* out on me.'

'That wasn't premeditated, Sasha. It happened.'

'Stolen kisses are the sweetest,' she jeered, then raged off around the room, firing words back at him like a hail of shotgun pellets. 'You were eyeing me over the moment you entered my room. If I hadn't put the table between us and kept you talking, you would have tried something more much sooner. As it was, we almost ended up in bed. If I hadn't made you control yourself...'

'Dammit, Sasha, I was the one who pulled back! I didn't want to take advantage of you. I know what it's like after a long relationship breaks up. The feelings of worthlessness . . .'

'I have never felt worthless in my life. Do you hear me? Never! And don't tell me you were thinking of pulling back this morning. You were openly planning to have an affair with me.'

'Of course I want an affair with you. Any man would. It's not necessary to *plan* these things. They happen. People do it all the time. I wanted to know if you felt what I did. And what's more . . .' a dangerous glitter leapt into his eyes '. . . I think you do, Sasha. You feel it every bit as strongly as I do. And that's why you're reacting like this.'

'If you think I'm going to share you with a beautiful . . .'

'Cut that out. You know why I'm going through with this marriage. It has nothing to do with love or loving. It's to collect a piece of paper. . . .'

'What about the consummation?'

'I'll close my eyes and think of you.'

'How dare you! How dare you flaunt . . . ?'

'I'm trying to mend fences.'

'Too late. The horse has bolted.'

'Let's see if it has.' He started walking towards her, his eyes sizzling with intent. 'Everything you said to Elizabeth was a ploy, was it?'

'Mostly,' Sasha snapped. She headed for the door. She was not going to do battle with animal magnetism.

'You were *magnificent*, Sasha.'

He was using that voice on her again. And those blue eyes of his were dynamite. 'I despise you,' she flung at him.

'I'm falling in love.'

It halted Sasha momentarily. 'Go try that line on the beautiful Polish woman you've contracted to marry.' She doggedly resumed her retreat towards the door.

'I don't know why you're taking this so badly.' He looked genuinely puzzled, and frustrated, and exasperated. 'I've only done what I quite openly discussed with you when we met in the park.'

'Good for you. Go right ahead. See if I care.'

His hands reached out in appeal. 'I want to placate you. How was I to know you'd come back into my life and give me some of my greatest moments?'

'That's what men always do. Justify themselves. No matter what,' she shot at him scathingly.

'It's not as if Urszula will be living with me.'

Sasha reached the door and opened it. She cast one last furious look at Nathan Parnell. 'By all means use the law as you wish to sort out your problems, Nathan Parnell. Please leave me out of them in your future planning. I won't be your witness ever again. I won't be your lover. Ever. I won't be a pretend mother for Matt, either, because that will end up breaking my heart. So you'd better straighten him out, too. Then get to work on yourself.'

'I'm sorry.' He looked bereft.

She slammed the door shut behind her. To Sasha's mind, it was the metaphoric slamming of a lot of doors on things she was never going to think about again.

Bigamy, she thought in towering outrage as she stamped up the stairs to the nanny's quarters. It was no better than bigamy.

CHAPTER TEN

FOR the next few days Sasha saw very little of Nathan Parnell. Occasionally they passed in the foyer or hall. She bestowed a frosty, 'Good morning,' or 'Good afternoon,' on him, disdaining any answer to the provocative things he chose to say to her.

Matt did not visit the nursery. Marion Bennet offered to mind Bonnie whenever Sasha had to go into the city to search through the archives for the facts Hester wanted. Sasha usually came home to find Matt playing with Bonnie in the Bennets' apartment, but she let that pass without comment. It involved no emotional attachment for herself and she was sympathetic to the little boy's loneliness.

Hester Wingate remained true to the autocratic behaviour of their first meeting, but Sasha found herself enjoying the old lady's highly individual view of the world and its inhabitants.

Hester loved thoroughbred horses and bloodlines. Breeding them had made her fortune, which accounted for her predisposition to judge things from the stallion's point of view.

She was an amazingly colourful character, unique in Sasha's experience, brutally direct in all her opinions and beliefs and blithely dismissing anything she considered not worthy of her attention. She was the perfect antidote to any brooding over Nathan Parnell's perfidy. That was reason enough for Sasha to like being with her, but the liking quickly became genuine for Hester herself.

Sasha's first action, on Hester's behalf, was to obtain a copy of Seagrave Dunworthy's will at the probate office. The clauses Marion had told her about were there, almost verbatim. There was a lot more besides. There was no beneficiary called Parnell; no beneficiary called Wingate; no beneficiary called Maddox, or any other name that Sasha recognised. The tontine existed, but the money was all diverted to a series of trusts.

Apart from the task of digging up dirt on Seagrave Dunworthy and Hester's other associates, Sasha had to check all the dates in the tampered bible. These related to the Dawson family with five sons and eight daughters. It took Sasha many hours to gather every birth, marriage and death certificate, but it didn't solve the problem.

Most of the children, at one time or another, had had a valid reason for altering their ages upwards. Four of the girls married before they reached the age of consent, and two of the boys enlisted in the army for World War One before they reached the minimum age. There was no obvious way of telling what was cause and what was effect. Did the boys enlist in the army knowing they were under age, or did they genuinely believe in the dates in the bible? It was very puzzling.

Sasha was so bent on evading Nathan Parnell that she almost missed paying her rent between nine a.m. and the twelfth stroke of noon on Friday. It was only when Hester paid her for her work that she remembered. Hester immediately ordered Brooks, her chauffeur, to drive Sasha home again.

It seemed the height of irony to be racing the clock in a Rolls-Royce for the sake of paying ten dollars, but Sasha was mightily relieved when she made it home with five minutes to spare. She bolted into the foyer and ran straight into Nathan. He had just emerged from the library which was directly across the foyer from the lounge.

'Please get out of my way!' she cried. 'I have to pay my rent.'

'I paid it for you.'

She pulled out of his steadying grasp and tried to catch her breath. She glared at him uncertainly. 'Why did you do that? Don't tell me you still want me living here.'

His eyes were piercingly blue, projecting the same concentrated interest in her that had held her captive in the park. 'I want you to stay.'

'It won't do you any good,' she warned, holding out the ten-dollar note she'd had ready to give to Marion Bennet. 'I don't want to owe you anything.'

'As you wish,' he said, taking the note and pocketing it.

'Do you pay rent?' she asked bluntly, discomfited by the thought he might somehow be the owner of the house.

'Of course.'

'How much?'

'The full five guineas. Ten dollars fifty.'

Sasha frowned. He couldn't be the owner, yet he obviously had a say in who came here. Without him, neither the Bennets nor she and Bonnie would have benefited from Seagrave Dunworthy's strange terms about the house. Nathan had to have some connection to the owner.

'What does Marion do with the money?' she asked.

'It goes into a trust account. But there is something which is far more important that I'd like to discuss with you. Do you know how many days it is to Christmas, Sasha?'

It was the first week of December. Sasha hastily calculated the time, thankful she now had the income from Hester enabling her to buy Bonnie some lovely gifts for her first Christmas. 'Twenty-two days,' she answered, which gave her plenty of time to shop.

Nathan looked triumphant, as though he had scored a major victory. Sasha recollected that this was the longest conversation they'd had since Monday. Not that it was any great deep and meaningful communication.

'This might be the season of goodwill to all men,' Sasha observed acidly, 'but I'm reserving my goodwill for women. And not all of them, either.'

'I'd like you to come to a pre-Christmas party with me, Sasha,' he said, an eloquent appeal in his eyes sliding straight through her defences and worming its way into her heart.

'Whatever for?' she demanded testily, resenting the ease with which he affected her.

'Because your friendship and support mean a lot to me.'

He sounded genuine. He looked genuine. Sasha couldn't ignore the fact he'd given her a lot of support when she was in desperate need of it. This home. Her job. 'Is it a special occasion?' she asked warily.

'It's not something I can pass up without giving offence. The judge has been like a father to me and——'

'What happened to your real father?' Sasha had become very curious about bloodlines.

'He fell off his horse in a polo game and broke his neck. I never really knew him.'

Horses again, Sasha thought.

'All my friends will be there, Sasha...'

She wouldn't mind seeing what his friends were like.

'...and they're aware of the custody case coming up. They know what Elizabeth is like. I'd rather not have to listen to sympathetic comments all night. If you'd come with me...'

His mention of the custody case and Elizabeth snapped Sasha out of her treacherous musing. 'Why don't you take the beautiful Polish woman you're going to marry?'

'Because I can't bear to be with her,' he said evenly.

Sasha was fascinated. 'Then you've made a poor choice of wife, haven't you?' she said silkily. 'When have you contracted to marry?'

'Next Wednesday.'

'Well, you've made your bed, Nathan. I don't think you have any option but to lie in it,' she said with some asperity.

'Sasha, I've tried to break that contract. I can't. I've never felt so desperate in my life. There's no way out.'

He certainly looked harassed, but Sasha was wary of accepting anything at face value. 'How have you tried?' She needed details.

'I lined up twenty different males who were prepared, with some inducements, to marry her in my place. Urszula is demanding specific performance from me. She won't be bought out of it and I can't find a substitute she'll accept.'

Urszula knew a good thing when she saw it, Sasha surmised, and was hanging on for more than Nathan had bargained for.

'The problem is I wrote the contract myself,' he continued. Sasha thought she heard a hint of desperation in his voice. 'It runs about five lines. It's in simple English. And there's no escape clause anywhere. I thought I was binding Urszula. Now it's me who's caught.'

'I told you in the park that what you proposed to do was not a well-thought-out arrangement. Love comes first. Then the marriage.'

'I fervently agree with you. I rather like your more direct approach. You're not selfish or grasping. Quite the contrary.'

Not exactly selfless, Sasha mentally corrected him. She didn't want to interrupt when he was speaking so well.

'There's so much I find admirable about you, Sasha. Others will admire you, too. We should get to know each other better. Having you at my side tomorrow night...it's a first step. It would commit you to nothing, Sasha, and I promise you'll have a good time. Let's have one night together.'

It was similar to granting one last favour to a condemned man. Nathan had certainly done her some favours. It ill behove her to refuse him this simple boon. Besides, it was a long time since she had let her hair down and had a good night out.

Nathan wasn't married yet. Perhaps...

'All right. Just this once,' she said with pointed emphasis. Sasha didn't want him to get any wrong ideas about what this party might lead to between them.

He gave her a sparkling smile that danced down Sasha's spine and hit her solidly in the solar plexus. 'I'll make the arrangements with Marion to mind the children.'

He was off before she could have second thoughts.

The second thoughts came anyway.

It was quite safe to go with him. Nothing would happen unless she wanted it to happen. But it was living dangerously.

CHAPTER ELEVEN

SASHA knew she shouldn't wear the red satin evening dress. It was strapless. It was figure-hugging. It had a slit up the centre seam at the back of the skirt for ease of movement, but there wasn't a man alive who wouldn't see that slit as provocative.

Tyler had chosen the dress. His professional eye admired dramatic effect. With Sasha's pale skin, her thickly lashed dark eyes and long black hair, her above average height and her fair share of feminine curves, the red satin dress delivered dramatic effect. It could be said . . . with oomph.

It was almost certainly wrong to wear it to a judge's Christmas party. The women there would probably be in black or cream or white, all understated class but extremely elegant and expensive. Not that the red satin dress was cheap. It wasn't. But it wasn't subtle. It was, to put it succinctly, a traffic-stopper.

What did it matter, Sasha reasoned to herself, if she raised eyebrows or drew stares tonight? She didn't know the people who would be at the party. She would probably never meet them again. She could please herself without any regard to what others thought, taking a leaf out of Hester's book and not caring a fig.

She had the right to be colourful. She was free to do as she liked. No obligation to anyone. Committed to nothing. That was what Nathan had said. He had also said she would look stunning in red.

Sasha had to admit to a deep primitive urge to stun his socks off. It would teach him a lesson for getting tied up with his Polish woman and not waiting for her. As for thinking she would have an affair with him, he had been undeceived on that matter in no uncertain terms when she'd told him she wanted love and commitment.

Sasha took another look at herself in the mirror. She *was* playing with fire. She *was* living dangerously. The cautious, common-sense side of Sasha knew all along she shouldn't wear the red satin evening dress. The devil made her do it.

The arrangement was that she meet Nathan in the foyer at eight o'clock. She didn't go down the back stairs. She had left Bonnie with Marion an hour ago, bathed, fed, and ready for sleep. This was her one night with Nathan before he married, and Sasha saw every reason to get full value out of it **right** from the start. She heard the grandfather clock in the foyer strike the first of eight strokes as she reached the head of the grand staircase.

He was waiting for her.

The clock tolled again as she stared at him. The note seemed to reverberate through her heart.

He was dressed in a formal black dinner suit, black bow-tie, white dress shirt. Why men always looked their most handsome and distinguished in such clothes, Sasha didn't know. All thought processes halted. Nathan Parnell was *stunning*.

He glanced up and saw her. An involuntary look of sheer wonderment passed over his face. He turned towards her, slowly, as though he might be deprived of a life-promising mirage if he wasn't careful. A hand lifted, impulsively reaching out its invitation to come to him. His vivid blue eyes consumed her.

Sasha had the sensation of floating down the stairs. She was barely aware of her legs moving. She reached the foot of the staircase and Nathan was there to meet her, and she put her hand in his, and there was silence for several dream-like moments, silence except for the swirl of feelings that whispered dreams could come true.

'Stunning,' he said simply.

'Thank you.'

'You've already made it a night to remember.'

As gratifying as that statement was, it brought Sasha back to reality. 'You'll have plenty of nights to reflect on that,' she reminded him pertly.

'All the more reason to live for the moment,' he replied, not the least bit abashed as he took her arm and tucked it around his.

It was the gentlemanly way to escort her to the car, Sasha reasoned, so she let him get away with it. However, she was intensely aware of him matching his steps to hers, his closeness, their togetherness. She could even smell his aftershave lotion. Somehow it was sexy, too; spicy, enticing and very male.

Once in the car, Sasha decided talk was the only way to ward off the animal magnetism that was gathering force by the second. Silence definitely had the effect of feeding it.

'Tell me about the people I'm going to meet at the party,' she said brightly.

Nathan was slow to answer. Sasha surmised that it was taking him a few moments to concentrate his mind. 'Judges, lawyers, layabouts, the rich, the poor, the famous, the infamous. They'll all be there. A cross section of society.'

It was a very general reply. Sasha had meant him to be more specific with names and character sketches. 'I thought you didn't like judges,' she remarked.

'On a continuing downward spiral,' he replied with feeling. 'There's not one of them, not *one*, who would find in my favour to break the contract with Urszula Budna. They were unanimously unhelpful. I know, because I checked them all.'

'You can't do that! Trying to solicit favours from judges!'

'Desperation,' he agreed. 'Anyway, it didn't work. Not one of them could find a loophole anywhere.'

So the marriage was inevitable.

Depression closed around Sasha's heart. She felt sorry for Nathan, sorry for herself, sorry for the shutting off of what might have been possible between them. A sense of futility in the evening ahead of them stirred a surge of rebellion. None of this was her fault. She had to get on with her own life.

'I have no sympathy for the mess you've got yourself into, Nathan. Self-inflicted,' she tartly reminded him. 'And I'm not going to carry a long face around with me all night. I'm going to enjoy myself.'

'If the primary function of a young woman is to leave a trail of devastated male hearts in her wake, you should enjoy yourself. Immensely,' he said with a touch of heavy irony.

'Enjoy myself I will, but not at the expense of others.'

Apparently he had no comeback to that. Sasha could feel him looking at her, willing her to look at him, but she kept her gaze fixed on the traffic ahead.

'I think it's the love in your heart that puts the bloom in your cheeks, the light in your eyes. It irradiates your person, Sasha, giving you a beauty that——'

'Please stop this nonsense.'

'I don't mind admitting I'm falling in love with you. What's your problem?'

Urszula Budna, Sasha thought savagely, but she wasn't about to admit anything. In the circumstances, any admission would not lead anywhere good. 'This is the most useless conversation I've ever had. I'd rather talk about the weather.'

Nathan lapsed into silence, obviously declining to wax lyrical about the weather although it was the kind of night made for lovers. Sasha was acutely aware of that when they reached their destination and she stepped out of the car. A full moon was rising. It was a cloudless starry sky. The air was warm and balmy with the sensual pleasure of a feathering breeze off the harbour.

They hadn't travelled far. Sasha was not surprised to find that Nathan's paternal judge lived in what could only be called a stately home. Like Seagrave

Dunworthy's mansion, and Hester Wingate's luxurious Mediterranean-style villa, it stood on a large
chunk of prime real estate which had been moulded by
expert gardeners into a splendid setting. It was nothing more than another extraordinary part of Nathan
Parnell's extraordinary life, Sasha thought flip-
pantly, refusing to be impressed.

There was even a parking attendant to remove and
take care of the BMW. That was indicative of what
was to come. Sasha held her head high as Nathan es-
corted her inside. Nothing and no one was going to
intimidate her tonight. She was as good as anyone else
and a darned sight better than some.

Her confidence was given a boost by their host's
reception. The venerable judge was well into his six-
ties but there was nothing jaded about his appreciation of Sasha. Having warmly welcomed her, he raised
enquiring eyebrows at Nathan.

'I had an idea that might help.'

'Yes?' Nathan encouraged.

'Change your religion. Become a Mormon.'

Having delivered this opinion, the judge turned to
greet other incoming guests.

Nathan looked quizzically at Sasha. 'That might
solve the problem.'

'*If* you can find a woman who won't mind sharing
a husband,' Sasha remarked sweetly, 'you're welcome to her.'

'I thought as much,' Nathan muttered darkly.
'You're not at all helpful.'

That was the limit of their private conversation.
Nathan was hailed by friends and they were quickly

drawn into a congenial group of people. Most of the introductions floated into Sasha's ears and out again. Too many names to remember. She was met with speculative interest, of one kind or another, from both men and women.

The men tended to envy Nathan, and the women envied her. It was good for Sasha's ego, yet it was an empty satisfaction. She didn't really *have* Nathan, and she didn't really *want* other men's interest.

Nevertheless, Sasha sparkled as she had never sparkled before. She drank French champagne. She nibbled gourmet delicacies from silver trays. Dinner-jacketed waiters circulated with endless supplies of tempting treats and Sasha in her red satin evening dress was definitely not a neglected guest.

She received charming care and attention, flirtatious care and attention, bold and purposeful care and attention. Nathan, however, seemed oblivious to all this. *His* care and attention was faultlessly courteous. Nothing more, nothing less.

Sasha found herself fuming with frustration. Nathan concentrated his interest on the conversations directed towards him. The women who drew that sexy focus of attention in those riveting blue eyes lapped it up and did their utmost to retain it. Men seemed to lobby for his approval. They all, men and women alike, basked in Nathan Parnell's personal charisma.

Sasha finally decided she had had enough. She bestowed her best brilliant smile on a notorious gambler who whisked her off to the ballroom and propositioned her as he demonstrated some blatantly suggestive dance steps. She didn't know whether to be flattered or outraged. In the end, she laughingly parried his wicked but good-humoured banter.

It reminded her of her resolution to enjoy herself. Emboldened by the gambler's success at removing Sasha from Nathan's side, other men asked her to dance with them. No objection came from Nathan and Sasha danced her feet off, gaily accepting invitation after invitation. She bubbled with vivacity. Every time her partners returned her to Nathan she glowed with the pleasure they had given her. Nathan smiled indulgently. He did not ask her to dance with him. He appeared to be having a perfectly fine time without her at his side.

Having got this heartburning message, Sasha danced on without bothering to return to his side. She didn't need *him*, either. There were plenty of men flocking around her, panting for her attention and lapping up every responsive flash in *her* eyes. There were men ready to get her another glass of champagne, men ready to please her palate with whatever food she might fancy, men hanging on every delightfully bubbly word that spilled from her red satin lips.

It was highly irritating to Sasha that such an idyllic situation should become extremely tiresome. But it did. She took the only possible relief that pride allowed her. She retreated to the ladies' powder-room and did some quiet seething while she ostensibly repaired her make-up.

Nathan Parnell was no more falling in love with her than the man in the moon. He hadn't even bothered to try taking her out to the romantic patio beyond the ballroom to show her the moon.

Matt was definitely wrong about his daddy's being able to do anything. Nathan Parnell had either resigned himself to defeat, or didn't care enough to compete for her undivided attention. Sasha was disappointed in him. Deeply disappointed.

Since her 'good time' had worn thin, and Nathan obviously didn't require her, Sasha saw no point in staying at the party any longer. She hoped Nathan would have the good manners to take her home upon request. If not, she would order a taxi. She was about to sally forth from the powder-room with this purpose in mind when she was confronted by the last woman in the world she wanted to see.

Elizabeth Maddox.

Nathan's ex-wife effectively blocked Sasha's exit with a stance that exuded haughty scorn. Sasha returned a bored look that hid quite a few explosive little questions—like whether Nathan had known Elizabeth was going to be here, and had he planned on using Sasha's presence to camouflage his real marriage plans from his litigious ex-wife?

'You don't look Polish,' Elizabeth opened up with gimlet-eyed suspicion.

'You don't look like a piranha,' Sasha retorted.

'So, Urzsula Budna thinks she has teeth, does she?' Elizabeth gave Sasha's dress a contemptuous once-over before lifting pitying eyes. 'Well, from tonight's performance, my dear, they're certainly not sunk into Nathan. That's why you've been playing up to every other man.'

This was clearly a case of mistaken identity and Sasha was tempted to blow Nathan's strategy wide open. He hadn't done the decent thing by her. He hadn't even done the indecent thing. He had been totally, callously and recklessly indifferent.

'You really want him and you can't get him,' Elizabeth sneered.

That goaded Sasha to resume battle stations. 'Sounds as if you're stating your own position,' she drawled, flicking her eyes over the sleek silvery gown her antagonist wore. 'A dead fish seems a more apt description than a piranha.'

Elizabeth resumed her haughty air. 'I had Nathan precisely where I wanted him. You do not.'

Sasha couldn't let that pass. 'I like a man to simmer before bringing him to the boil. It's called living dangerously. But very exciting.'

Another woman entered the powder-room. Elizabeth had to step aside and Sasha seized the opportunity to leave. She headed straight for where she had last seen Nathan. He was engaged in some lively debate with a raven-haired beauty and a bunch of lawyers.

Sasha hooked her arm around Nathan's, flashed her teeth at his companions, then brought their discussion to a dead halt.

'Please excuse us, ladies and gentlemen. Nathan needs to dance with me. His legs might get broken if he doesn't do it right now.'

'She Who Must Be Obeyed,' Nathan intoned, but without resistance.

They all laughed.

Nathan swept Sasha away towards the ballroom, stroking her arm as though she was a ruffled cat that required soothing. She didn't purr. As far as she was concerned, fur was about to fly.

'To what do I owe the honour?' he asked, a silky satisfaction in his voice.

'Don't get tickets on yourself,' Sasha warned. 'You're a sneaky rotten scoundrel who'll say anything that'll give you an advantage.'

He gave her a hurt look. 'When have I not spoken the truth to you, Sasha?'

'Falling in love with me,' she scoffed at him, 'was a villainous lie.'

'Undeniable fact.' He swung her into his arms as they reached the dance floor. 'Feel my heart. It's almost bursting with the excitement of holding you close to me.'

She declined the invitation, her eyes flashing dark scorn. 'Why didn't you ask me to dance with you?'

'I was respecting your wishes regarding freedom of action.'

'What wishes?'

'Not to be with me. To enjoy yourself with others,' he answered blandly.

'I didn't say that.'

The blue eyes lit with hope and devilish desire. 'You mean I misunderstood? You wanted to enjoy yourself with me? I could have danced all night with you? You wouldn't have refused if I asked?'

The arm around her waist pressed her closer. He executed a turn that frotted their thighs together in a highly intimate manner. A dangerous current of warmth raced through Sasha.

'The only reason I'm dancing with you now is to show your ex-wife I can have you any time I want,' she gritted.

'You can,' he assured her with fervour. 'I can't sleep at night for thinking of how it would be between us. I want you so much . . .'

Sasha stamped on his foot to concentrate his mind on the real burning issue. 'She's here! And you knew she was going to be here, didn't you?'

'Who?'

'Elizabeth!'

'Do you know how tantalising it is when your breasts heave like that? Irresistible. I feel . . .'

'Your ex-wife is watching us,' Sasha almost yelled at him in frustration.

'Put your arms around my neck. Let's give her some dirty dancing. I can do it with you. Elizabeth won't be left in any doubt about how deeply you stir me.'

She glowered at him as she followed his suggestion. 'Not too dirty. I don't want you getting pleasure out of your trickery, Nathan Parnell.'

'I promise that whatever happens, I won't be pleased. I also swear to you I didn't know Elizabeth would be here,' he said solemnly, his eyes burning into hers. 'I do know she wasn't invited. She must be with another guest.'

Sasha cogitated on that statement for several moments. Nathan made it very difficult for her to concentrate. Full body contact, and the way he was making the most of it, was extremely distracting. His expertise in dancing not only left nothing to be desired, it flowed and pulsed with a sexuality that was stimulating a lot of other desires.

Surely he would have been doing this before if he'd known Elizabeth was here. Being a stand-offish escort didn't fit the scenario of trying to keep the wool pulled over his ex-wife's eyes. Sasha had to concede it was more probable that she had leapt to a false conclusion. Nathan Parnell was not guilty as she had charged him.

'Elizabeth thinks I'm your Polish woman,' she said. 'She knows about Urszula Budna.'

'Marriage application forms. She'd do a check to make sure we're really getting married.'

'But I'm not Urszula Budna.'

He gave her a heart-melting smile. 'I know. Thank you, Sasha.'

She struggled against melting. 'What for?'

'Thumbing your nose at Elizabeth. Sticking by me again in spite of your reservations.'

'I can't abide people like her,' she defended.

'You have great principles. An admirable mind. A generous heart. A beautiful body.'

He was screwing them all up with what he was doing in this dance, Sasha thought, torn between the need to keep fighting him and the need to give in to the pleasure of simply feeling him and the feelings he stirred in her.

Elizabeth was watching, she told herself, and that was justification enough to act with a certain amount of uninhibited élan. She wriggled a little closer. Nathan's hands slid to her hips, swaying her into a seductive rhythm that was definitely dirty. It aroused more than a simmer of excitement.

'Stop it,' she hissed.

He bent his head, his warm breath tingling her ear as he whispered. 'I want to, but I can't. Do you know how erotic you feel in this dress?'

She had known all along that she shouldn't have worn it.

'It's so sensual,' he murmured huskily. 'So hot, so vivid, so *you*.'

'Dance me out to the patio.'

'Great idea!'

'It's cooler out there,' Sasha suggested, acutely aware of her own heated response to the hardness pressing into her stomach.

'Let's leave. I don't want to be with anyone else but you.'

'Nathan . . .' Her voice quivered and died. She was suddenly breathless, confused by the strength of her own desire to have him to herself. Before she could make up her mind whether to stay in the safety of numbers or go with him, he whirled her down to the end of the ballroom, his legs imprisoning hers in a rhythm that was too intensely exciting to break.

He scythed through the crowd with purposeful haste, scooping Sasha along with him, stopping for no one, only pausing at the front door to ask someone to order his car to be brought immediately. Then they were outside, and in the intoxication of the moment Nathan swept Sasha up in his arms and carried her down the steps to the driveway. There he let her slide to her feet, moulding the pliant softness of her body to his rampant virility as he kissed her with a devouring passion that Sasha was powerless to resist.

She didn't hear the car pull up beside them. She didn't hear its doors being opened. Her heart thundered in her ears, her head swam with dizzying sensations, her body revelled in the wild pulse of desire that beat from him to her in throbbing waves. She had never known anything like it.

Nathan lifted her into the passenger seat. He fastened the seatbelt for her. His lips roved over hers, reluctant to break the thrall of sensuality. She heard his sharp intake of breath as he pulled back. Her door was shut. She watched in a daze as he strode quickly to the driver's side. Then he was beside her, revving the engine, accelerating them on their way, and his hand took possession of hers, fingers interlacing, gripping, wanting so much more.

A voice in the back of Sasha's mind told her she'd better think about this and think fast.

But she didn't want to think.

This was a time for doing.

CHAPTER TWELVE

IT WAS going up the stairs that dispelled Sasha's pleasurable haze of anticipation for what would happen next. If Nathan had carried her, she might still have clung to feeling swept away from any thought of tomorrow. The mechanical act of placing one foot after another beat home the knowledge that each step took her closer to Nathan's bedroom, and there was no commitment to anything other than satisfying the need burning through both of them.

He was still gripping her hand.

As they reached the top of the stairs she halted, turning to him with wary, accusing eyes. 'It's the dress, isn't it? I shouldn't have worn it.'

He touched her cheek with tenderness. 'It's not the dress. It's the woman inside it.'

'But...'

'We'll soon get rid of the dress. Then you can see for yourself.'

He headed for the nanny's quarters, drawing her after him, making any protest about proceeding with him untenable. He was leading her to *her* door.

'You're going to marry another woman,' she said, but even to her own ears her voice failed to carry much conviction.

'I'm not married yet.'

'How can you possibly get *out* of the contract?'

He looked sternly into her eyes. 'Suicide is always a good last alternative.'

It was no alternative as far as Sasha was concerned. Nathan was so vital, so... attractive in every way. The thought of him dead put a queasy hollowness in her stomach. She wanted him, wanted him for herself, and the prospect of never having him suddenly made a wasteland of her future life.

He opened the door to her bed-sitting-room.

She hesitated. Was she ready to commit herself to an uncertain fate with him? 'Maybe we should...'

The blaze of desire in his eyes seared the thought from her mind. 'Now,' he said with a deep throb of passion. 'This is the moment we've both been waiting for. The moment of truth.'

Sasha knew there was something wrong with that statement, although there was something right in it, too. Before she could identify the flaws in the argument that would clarify what she should or shouldn't do, Nathan manoeuvred her into the danger area and she was in his arms with the door shut behind them.

He kissed her.

It fuzzed up her mind very badly. She had the sensation of her legs moving backwards, being pushed along by piston-like thighs, but there was a lot of other sensational things happening so she wasn't absolutely sure about that until she toppled on to the bed and found herself underneath the man who was still kissing her, trailing a hot, hungry mouth down her throat, cutting off her breath, making her feel giddy with his ardour.

'I drank too much champagne. Otherwise I wouldn't be letting you do this,' she gasped out, trying to explain the strong urge to unrestrained wantonness that was pumping through her body.

'More champagne,' he breathed in her ear. 'That's what we need. More champagne.'

He started to move away from her. She pulled him back because she didn't think she could handle any more champagne, not when she should be trying to think of other things. Nathan misunderstood. His mouth ravished hers with increasing intensity, kissing her again and again, excitement escalating into a writhing desire that was frustratingly restricted by their clothes.

Nathan suddenly raised himself, straddling her as he tore his arms out of his jacket and hurled it on to the floor. A sobering splash of reality gave Sasha the strength to make one last effort against committing herself to the unknown.

'Let's not be too hasty about this, Nathan,' she pleaded, uncertain whether the point of no return had already been passed in making up her mind as to what she should, or should not do.

'You're right.' His eyes had a feverish glitter. 'I don't want to be tempted into taking you prematurely. We should have the pleasure of slowly undressing each other, being naked together.'

'That's not what I meant.'

'It's what I meant. I'll do the tricky bits first.'

He pushed his cufflinks free and tossed them in the same direction as the jacket. Then he started on his bow-tie. The pressure of his loins had her pinned to the bed. The heat of his body, the controlled strength of his thighs, the promise of seeing him as all raw male, made a heady intoxicant for Sasha. She didn't really want to move, but there was a niggle in the back of her mind that wouldn't go away.

'I won't have you *taking* me,' she said more strongly.

'Wrong label. Politically incorrect. Forgive the expression.' He flashed her a wicked grin. 'I want you to take me, too. All of me.'

That conjured up tantalising images. Her stomach contracted excitedly, warningly, as he discarded the bow-tie and proceeded to undo the studs of his dress-shirt.

'What do you think you're doing?' she croaked.

'Taking my clothes off. Better to get them out of the way. Frustrating otherwise.'

'You can do that in your own bedroom,' Sasha said shrilly. The glimpse of bare skin from the gape in the fabric made naked fact of fantasy, and what if he didn't feel the same about her as she did about him? What if...?

Again came the grin that undermined any train of reason. 'No novelty in that. Done it many times before. If you'd like to help me...'

'No!' She swallowed hard. 'I think we should talk sensibly about this, Nathan.'

He raised a quizzical eyebrow. 'When it's your turn I won't use any hands to undress you. Just my mouth, teeth, lips and tongue. What do you think of that?'

Her mind boggled. Could he do it? 'But this doesn't solve anything,' she wailed somewhat desperately as he shed his shirt and threw it on to the ever-growing pile.

'My word it does, Sasha. It solves a lot of things,' he replied fervently.

He had a torso that would make any woman go cross-eyed. Sasha was no exception. It was not often one saw a splendid arrangement of muscle, skin and bone. Her impression in the park was absolutely correct. A perfectly proportioned lover.

It's not human to resist, she argued to herself, and Nathan was right. It would solve a lot of things. Like knowing instead of wondering. Tentatively she reached out, stroking her fingers over the flesh from the waist up. He flinched and she could see the muscle spasm under her touch. It made her feel... powerful. Nathan had his little sensitivities, as well. She could touch him and... On a wave of wild exhilaration she put the tips of her stroking fingers into her mouth and sucked them.

'You taste good.'

He laughed joyously as he raised himself on to his knees. His hands unfastened the waistband of his trousers. The zipper followed. 'Now you can do it all the way over me.'

Her eyes widened at the bulge in his underpants. He looked so... *big*. Her mind fluttered to Tyler. She had never been intimate with any other man. She couldn't

remember feeling so . . . mesmerised . . . by the sight of
Tyler. Nathan was different. Nathan was enticingly
different, excitingly different, magnificently different. And he certainly wanted her as much as, if not
more than, she wanted him.

Her hands moved to draw his trousers down, to see,
to know, to touch. He leaned over her and ran his
tongue over the swell of her breasts above the bodice
line of her dress. ''You taste good, too,'' he murmured. Then his teeth closed over the edge of satin and
tugged.

Good heavens! she thought, he's really going to do
it. Undress me without using his hands.

'There's a zip at the back.'

'I'll get to it.'

'You'll need help. You can't do this by yourself.'
The strapless bodice was boned to mould around her
breasts and it was impossible to tug it down without
undoing the zipper first.

'Trust me. I can do it,' he growled, having moved
the satin enough to dip his tongue into her cleavage,
making her impatient to feel the hot, tingling caress on
her nipples. What would he make her feel when he
reached them?

'You undressed yourself with the tricky bits,' she
argued.

'True.'

'It'll be better if I undress myself.'

He sighed. 'If you must.'

'Stand up for a moment.'

He moved swiftly, unpinning her. He was off the
bed, ridding himself of the last of his clothes before

Sasha found enough presence of mind to sit up. What she saw made her breath catch in her throat, made her temples pulse with a roaring of blood. Her mind glazed with the wonder of taking all of him. An experience, she thought, a once-in-a-lifetime experience no woman in her right mind would pass up. Even if it was wrong.

She swung herself off the bed, turning away from him so she wouldn't be caught staring. He was tearing off his shoes and socks. Her legs felt quivery. Her hands were tremulous. She fumbled over the hook and eye. She finally managed to get it apart, grabbed the head of the zipper and scorched it down her back.

As the red satin slid off her body to pool at her feet, Sasha heard Nathan's sharp intake of breath, knew they were definitely beyond the point of no return now, and didn't care. A wild exultation filled her mind as she stepped away from the dress and turned to face what was to come.

For this one night I'll do anything I want, anything I like, she thought, casting off all the inhibiting shadows that might encroach on the blissful sense of freedom. She had wanted Nathan Parnell almost from the first moment they met, and the wanting had increased with everything he'd done for her, everything he was. If she never had him again, she would have him tonight.

He stared at her, his eyes feasting on what she had bared for him. 'Perfect breasts,' he groaned, stepping closer to cup them in his hands. The warmth of his palms and the caress of his fingers felt perfect to Sasha.

She ran her hands up his arms, over his shoulders, revelling in the naked strength that was bared to her. He felt like polished wood, hard and satiny smooth, but he was warmly, wonderfully alive. His hands suddenly slid around her back, pulling her into an urgent embrace, flattening the soft pliant fullness of her breasts against his chest, flooding her body with the throbbing heat of his. His fingers raked her pantihose down, clearing the curve of her bottom so he could fill his hands with its roundness and press her into an even more intimate awareness of his arousal.

'You're too excited!' she exclaimed.

'Disagree.'

He had no time for words. He bent to roll the sheer nylon down her thighs and his mouth closed over one of her breasts, and he used his lips, tongue, teeth, with such exquisite eroticism that Sasha thought she would die from the pleasure of it. She grasped his head and forced it to her other breast, wanting to feel it there, too. She lifted her leg so he didn't have to move away to complete the removal of the stocking. He took her shoe with it. The other leg. The other breast.

Please. More. Yes, yes, yes. She didn't know if she said the words or whether they simply pulsed through her. Free of the other stocking and shoe, his hand sliding between her thighs. Yes, there, too, yes, yes, and he did it with caring softness, sweet blissful caresses along the sensitive folds, soothing and exciting, more and more exciting, an arc of vibrating excitement from her breasts to the rhythmic plunging of his fingers, but fingers weren't enough. She wanted . . .

'Nathan...' Her hands clawed at his back, tugged at his head, frantic with urgency.

He responded with a surge of strength, lifting her, sliding the hard power of his virility to the centre of her need. She coiled her legs around his waist, leaned back, and moaned with ecstatic relief as she felt the massive force of him enter her, filling her, pushing past the convulsive spasms of muscles that closed and expanded around him, reaching further, further, stretching for...

'Let go, Sasha. Let go.'

Her mind was in chaos, unknowing what he meant. Her legs were locked around him. She couldn't let him go...except her arms. She let them slide limply from his neck and he caught her securely as she fell back, supporting her bottom and waist. And he began rotating like a ballet dancer in a spin. She stretched out her arms, her hair floating as he turned and turned...a carousel of throbbing intimacy, the connection deeply inside, undulating, all of him, all of her.

There was a sharp tingling through her skin as the blood drained into her torso, her face, her head. It was dizzying, intoxicating. The room was going around and around with the beat of his thrusting maleness, a pump of pleasure deep within her, strong and constant as she floated around it, melted around it, shattered into a million exploding pieces around it.

Then he caught her to him and laid her back on the bed, stacking pillows under her so she didn't need his support, and his hands were free to stroke her in harmony with the stroking within. An erotic feather-touch under her hipbones as he slid forward, a light palm pressure on her stomach as he deepened the thrust, the uplifting capture of her breasts as he drove to the end, then all the way back again with the mind-blowing anticipation of the next slow plunge, and the next.

It was beautiful, enthralling, hypnotic in its repetitive pattern, yet the desire to touch him stirred Sasha to lift her heavy arms, reach out, capture his face. It broke his concentration. His eyes met hers and they stared at each other in dazed wonderment. She pulled his head down and kissed him with all the love and yearning for oneness with the mate of her heart and mind and soul. The uninhibited outpouring of her passion shattered his control. She felt his body start to tremble.

He tore his mouth away. 'Sasha . . .' It was a hoarse breath of need. 'Sasha . . .' An acknowledgement of what she did to him.

She found the strength to rock with him as he frenziedly sought the fulfilment of release. It came with a great shuddering cry from him, and again it was 'Sasha . . .' like a bursting dam of feeling that could not be contained any more.

She did not know if it was a moment of truth. She wrapped her arms around him and held him close. She didn't speak. Her feelings went beyond words. But her heart beat its own refrain . . . Nathan . . . Nathan . . .

CHAPTER THIRTEEN

A LOUD rap on her door stirred Sasha from deep sleep. She found herself half sprawled over Nathan whose eyes were closed, but, as she started to move, his arm instinctively curled more firmly around her.

'Sasha, are you awake?'

Marion Bennet's raised voice was a clear call to attention. The thought of Bonnie jerked Sasha up with a guilty start. How late was it?

'Whass wrong?' Nathan slurred sleepily.

'Hush!' She clamped a hand over his mouth, her heart galloping at the thought of Marion walking in on them.

'Sasha?' Another louder knock.

Sasha managed a reply. 'Yes. Hold on a moment. I'm coming.'

Nathan heaved himself up on one elbow as she hurtled out of bed and ran to the wardrobe. He watched with a smile as she quickly wrapped herself in the turquoise silk robe. She frowned a warning at him, and he kept a discreet silence as she went to the door.

Mindful of the chaos of clothes on the floor, not to mention the man in her bed, Sasha squeezed around the door, carefully blocking any view past her as she addressed Nathan's housekeeper.

'Sorry I slept late, Mrs Bennet. I'll come and get Bonnie now.'

'She's fine, dear. Harry and Matt are playing with her out in the back garden. It's your visitors. I wasn't sure what to do about them. So I'm checking with you first.'

'Visitors?' Sasha hadn't expected anyone to call on her, except perhaps her parents, and they would telephone first. 'Who are they?'

'A Mr Cullum and a Mr McDougal.'

Tyler and Joshua! What did they want? 'I'd better get dressed.'

'Will I ask them in?'

'No!' Her emphatic refusal startled Marion. Sasha quickly tempered her voice. 'I'll go and talk to them, Mrs Bennet. Did you leave them waiting on the portico?'

Marion nodded. 'It wasn't polite but I had orders not to let anyone harass you.'

Sasha didn't have to ask where the orders came from. He was in her bed. 'I'll get dressed and go down to them straight away.'

'Take your time and don't worry about Bonnie. When you're ready is soon enough,' Marion assured her.

Sasha whirled back into her room as the housekeeper headed for the back staircase. She shut the door, took a deep breath, then met Nathan's acute blue gaze.

'Who's McDougal?' he asked.

'Tyler's partner. They share a photographic studio.'

'What do they want?'

She shrugged to express her lack of knowledge.

'Is this trouble, Sasha?'

'I doubt it. Not with Joshua along.'

'I'll come with you.'

'No. *I'll* handle this. *You* clean up the evidence.'

She waved at the wild array of clothing on the floor. He grinned, the memory of last night's wild abandonment sparkling in his eyes. Her heart jiggled as though he had it on a yo-yo. Regretfully, it wasn't last night any more. It was tomorrow.

'I've got to get moving, Nathan.'

She hurried back to the wardrobe, grabbed some fresh clothes, and raced off to the bathroom. By the time she emerged, washed, hair brushed, clothed in jeans and T-shirt, Nathan was gone and the floor was swept clean of any reminder of their intimacy. She found the red satin evening dress hanging up. She didn't pause to wonder where he'd put the other telltale items.

As she hurried downstairs to meet the man who had shredded the trust she had given him, Sasha had to wonder if she had committed the ultimate foolishness in succumbing to her feelings for Nathan Parnell. Whatever the outcome of their union, it was done now. At least her relationship with Tyler was well and truly resolved. She had no regrets about leaving him and had no desire or intention of ever going back to him.

If he had brought Joshua along to act as his advocate in a reconciliation, she had to make it absolutely clear there would be no future for them, except for

Tyler's rights as Bonnie's father. Despite this resolution, Sasha opened the front door with some trepidation. Tyler was a man of many moods, most of them volatile. Initially his uninhibited responses had been a source of attraction. Somewhere along the line they had become self-indulgently excessive.

They weren't on the portico. They were both at the foot of the steps, leaning against a huge king-of-the-road four-wheel-drive Range Rover, complete with bull bars and insect screens. It was not the kind of vehicle Sasha would have readily associated with Tyler, but apparently he or Joshua had the use of it this morning.

Tyler was stern but Joshua had a smile for her, giving his characteristic gesture of peace and goodwill. The tension inside Sasha eased slightly. Joshua's long, loose-limbed body seemed permanently relaxed. Unruffled by anything, he presented the absolute contrast to Tyler's air of restless energy.

'Quite a step up, Sasha,' Tyler drawled derisively, casting a glance over the impressive façade of the house.

'How did you find me, Tyler?'

'Your parents gave me the address so I could write to you.' He gave a harsh bark of laughter. 'What's it like, living in a mansion?'

'The same as anywhere else. It's the people who count.'

'And I don't count any more.'

'Not in my life, Tyler. I'm not blaming you. We didn't fit together in the end.'

Tyler chewed that over in his mind. Then his face lightened and he jerked his head sideways. 'What do you think of *her*?'

Puzzled, Sasha looked about, trying to locate the female in question. No one in sight.

Tyler didn't notice. He slapped his hand down on the bull bar. 'When you walked out on me, I had to find a replacement. Josh and I pooled our resources and we bought this. We've named it *Mary Bryant*. How does that strike you?'

Replaced by a car, Sasha thought numbly. She couldn't trust herself to any words. She raised her arms slightly, opened the palms of her hands and heaved her shoulders. Let him make what he could of that expression of his inadequacy.

Tyler didn't notice that, either. 'We're off to the interior,' he declared with an air of triumph. 'Take the greatest photos ever taken. Coffee-table stuff. We won't be back for years. We might never come back.' He grinned at his partner. 'Will we ever come back, Josh?'

'Never,' Joshua agreed amiably.

Sasha had the strong sensation that this was all meant to be very vengeful and threatening from Tyler, but somehow it struck her as a great idea.

'I'm glad you're doing what you really want to do,' she said in a conciliatory tone. She did not want to part bad friends with Tyler. There might come a time when Bonnie wanted to know her father and Tyler did have an attractive side. It was responsibility that weighed him down.

'I do care for you and Bonnie,' he jerked out.

'I know that, Tyler,' she replied sadly, thinking of the wasted years. 'But you need your freedom.'

'You understand.'

'Yes, Tyler, I understand.'

She looked at Joshua with knowing eyes. His reflected the same knowledge. They both knew it was easier for Tyler to travel lightly without the burden of a wife and child. She looked back at Tyler and managed a generous smile.

'I hope this venture leads to all you ever wanted.'

'Yes ... well ... I have to admit it's a relief you've taken it like this, Sasha,' he acknowledged. 'We weren't getting on so well, but it made me feel inadequate for wanting to duck out on you and Bonnie.'

Sasha understood that, too. It was a question of pride and self-image. Tyler didn't like to feel badly about himself. No doubt it had driven him to the abortive attempt at reconciliation in the park, despite his desire to be free of any encumbrances.

'It's OK,' she assured him. 'It wasn't working for either of us. It's better we go our separate ways.'

'I'll pay you maintenance for Bonnie, Sasha. Josh convinced me I should. What we figured ...'

Tyler's voice trailed into silence. Both he and Joshua stared past her and she felt Nathan's presence like a force-field, generating potent elements that changed the *status quo*. The surprise on Tyler's face tightened into pugnacity.

'You! What the hell are you doing here?' Tyler demanded, his eyes furiously accusing Sasha of putting him in the wrong again.

'I live here,' Nathan answered blandly, and, much to Sasha's consternation, put his arm around her shoulders, laying claim to her, flooding her body with a hot awareness of his. Then to compound the possessive action, he asked, 'Can I help, darling?'

Tyler gave Nathan a scathing look. 'You're the cop who broke up my talk to Sasha in the park. If this is your home you must be the most corrupt cop in the whole damned police force. You've got to be worse than Shags Bordello, worse than . . .' He was lost for words.

Joshua eyed Sasha with some concern. 'If you've got yourself involved in something . . .'

'I left the police force after I won Lotto,' Nathan interrupted, explaining away the unexplainable.

'Some people have all the luck,' Tyler muttered bitterly. 'I've never won Lotto.'

'Precisely,' Nathan agreed.

Tyler turned truculently to Joshua. 'She's found a new lover. One that can supply her with more than I ever could. That's what's to blame.'

'Is that right, Sasha?' Joshua asked, not as ready as Tyler to leap to conclusions.

'Yes, it is,' Nathan confirmed before she could begin to defend herself against the accusation of being a heartless gold-digger. Her mouth opened and snapped shut in stupefied shock as Nathan rattled on.

'Absolutely correct. Expressed very succinctly. Sasha is much better off living with me. So is Bonnie. Took to me straight away. I always wanted a ready-made family.'

Tyler looked as if he was about to burst a blood vessel. 'I was trying to do the honourable thing,' he seethed. 'Now I've changed my mind. You're not getting one damned thing from me, Sasha. No maintenance. Nothing for the kid, either.'

'Hold hard there, Tyler,' Joshua said lazily. 'We haven't heard Sasha's side of this.'

'Not one cent! Let him look after her and his ready-made family. All my work. He's getting what he wants. All my hard work wasted.' With a dismissive wave of his hand, Tyler headed for the driver's side of the *Mary Bryant*.

Sasha recognised the futility of saying anything. Even if it was possible, it was too late to correct the impression Nathan had so deliberately and effectively imparted.

Tyler hurled himself into the driver's seat. Joshua threw up his hands and hurried to the passenger's side. Tyler was starting the engine when a white Porsche zipped into the driveway, passed the Range Rover, ducked in front of it, braked fiercely, and came to a gravel spitting halt.

Out whirled Elizabeth Maddox.

The expression on her face promised that revenge was sweet. She didn't so much as flick a look at the rumbling Range Rover. Her sleet grey eyes glittered at Sasha and Nathan as she strode between the two vehicles.

'I told you not to come here again, Elizabeth.' Nathan had steel in his voice.

It didn't stop her. She started mounting the steps, her arm sweeping up to point an accusing finger at

Sasha. 'She is not Urszula Budna, and don't think you're going to get away with fraud. Urszula Budna has come to see me. She is now my client.'

Nathan pretended to have a heart attack. Sasha didn't see anything humorous in that at all.

'I'll blow this case wide open,' Elizabeth crowed. She sneered at Sasha then intensified the sneer for Nathan. 'This mistress thing on the side. You're going to lose the custody case, as well. You are a walking disaster, Nathan. I'll strip you so bare, there won't even be any bones left for the carrion to peck out.'

Nathan's eyes narrowed. 'I think you're in for a spot of bother yourself, Elizabeth.'

'Don't be ridiculous. Nothing is going to hurt me. I even bought a new car to show my contempt for your behaviour. In fact...'

While Elizabeth was rebutting Nathan's opinion, Sasha watched in fascination as Tyler exited his vehicle and slowly ascended the steps behind Elizabeth. He tapped her on the shoulder, interrupting the spate of words flowing from Elizabeth's lips.

'You sprayed my car with gravel. You hit *Mary Bryant*.'

Elizabeth barely noticed the hiatus. 'Don't interrupt me while I'm speaking.'

'You got out of the wrong tree this morning,' Tyler said more menacingly.

'Please go away.'

'Aren't you going to apologise? Say you're sorry?'

'Will you please go away?'

'OK.'

Tyler walked back to the vehicle that was designed for hard work and hard living. Sasha breathed her relief. Then she saw what he was going to do as he reversed his new pride and joy, braked, and revved the powerful engine. She closed her eyes.

'Don't close your eyes while I'm talking to you,' Elizabeth fumed.

Sasha opened her eyes. The huge Range Rover charged forward. There was the sound of crashing metal as it rammed the back of the white Porsche. The rear end of the little car crumpled. The Porsche slewed to one side. Tyler reversed. He was going to ram it again in the side. Dazed, they all looked on helplessly as the bull bars bit into the driver's door, crunching it inwards, then trundled the whole car forward as though it were a smashed toy being bulldozed off to the scrapheap.

'That's my car!' Elizabeth screamed.

It was ear-piercing.

She forgot Nathan and Sasha, plunged down the steps, ran furiously to stop the metal carnage along the driveway, yelling unspeakable violence at the perpetrator. Not even the Pope could have found such words, even in prayer.

The Range Rover halted. Tyler reversed again.

'Stop it, stop it, stop it!' Elizabeth screeched.

It was already too late for that.

Tyler paused to lean his elbow on the window ledge of the driver's door and look down upon the perpetrator of the initial offence. 'Say you're sorry for hitting *Mary Bryant*.'

'Yes. No. I don't know.' It sounded as though Elizabeth had burst more than a blood vessel. She was having a cerebral haemorrhage.

Tyler put his foot on the accelerator.

'Yes. I'm sorry,' Elizabeth screamed. 'For God's sake! Don't do it again.'

The acceleration dropped to a throaty rumble. Tyler leaned out again, this time to give dictation. 'Say after me. "I'm sorry I hurt *Mary Bryant*."'

Elizabeth forced the words out. 'I'm...sorry... I...hurt...*Mary Bryant*.'

'If you'd said that earlier, it would have saved you a great deal of trouble. Let this be a lesson to you.'

Nathan and Sasha automatically strolled down to the driveway to survey the damage now that the worst appeared to be over. Elizabeth looked as though she was barely containing herself from flying at Tyler tooth and nail.

'And one more thing,' he said with a mocking leer. 'You didn't unman me one bit when you behaved like a bitch in heat between the sheets. I got the better of you there, too.'

Sasha closed her eyes. Had Elizabeth Maddox been another of Tyler's infidelities when he was taking photos for magazine articles on celebrities?

'You're nothing but an animal,' Elizabeth snarled.

'It takes one animal to recognise another.'

'Pig!'

'Sow!'

'Do I take it there's been some intimacy between you two?' Nathan slid in sweetly.

'One of your women on the side, Tyler?' Sasha asked.

Neither answered.

Tyler drove off, looking like an Olympic champion who had just received his gold medal.

'What happens to me?' Elizabeth wailed.

'I'll get Marion to call a taxi for you,' Nathan said dismissively.

'I can do that for myself,' Elizabeth snapped. 'I have a mobile phone.'

'Fine. We'll leave you to it.'

'Aren't you going to ask me in?'

'I think not,' Nathan said, completely unruffled.

He hooked Sasha's arm around his. They turned in unison and walked back up the steps. The last Sasha saw of Elizabeth was her isolated figure, surveying her wrecked Porsche and wringing her hands. She looked as if she could break into tears of frustration.

'We make a great couple, don't we?' Nathan said with ringing satisfaction as he closed the front door behind them.

'Do you still have to marry Urszula Budna?' Sasha asked, uncertain of where they stood after the latest development with Elizabeth, and the revelation of her affair with Tyler.

Nathan sighed. 'The contract survives, regardless of what Elizabeth did or did not do with Tyler.'

'So the situation remains the same.'

'No. We've got rid of Tyler for good now.'

Sasha frowned. 'Why did you interfere? He was going anyway. What you got rid of, Nathan, was any financial support for Bonnie.'

There was not one flicker of guilt in his eyes. 'If Bonnie is in need of anything, I'll fix it. Until such time as she can support herself.'

He was certainly an expert at fixing things, Sasha thought with heavy irony. He had been doing it for her ever since they'd met. If only they'd met sooner. Or after all the complications in his life had been sorted out. Why did she have to get involved with men who wouldn't or couldn't commit themselves to a straight line relationship?

'That's my commitment to you, Sasha,' Nathan said quietly, as though he had read her mind. 'I'll put it in writing if you like. Either way, I will look after you and Bonnie.'

The bittersweet assurance lifted some of the depression in her heart, but it didn't remove the one reality that dimmed any pleasure in thinking of a future together. 'In a few days, Urszula Budna will have more rights than she has now,' Sasha stated flatly.

'She has nothing to do with us, Sasha.' Nathan drew her into his arms, stirring memories of last night's soul-deep intimacy.

Sasha pressed her hands against his chest in protest at his power to swamp her with feeling. She lifted deeply vulnerable eyes to his. 'But you have to sleep with her to make the marriage safe against legal threat.'

'Nothing on this earth could make me do that after what we shared last night.'

'You really mean that?'

He smiled, a slow sensual smile that lit his eyes with a wicked sparkle. 'Let me show you,' he said, and pulled her into the library with him.

'Nathan, we can't——'

'We can.'

'The children——'

'Are being well looked after.'

'We mustn't——'

'Be long. OK. Time trial. Starting from now.'

He leaned her against the door and unfastened her jeans as he kissed her. Before Sasha knew what she was doing, her hands were active on his trousers. Desire was terribly consuming. Once it took hold, it took over. Time trials made it all the more exciting.

CHAPTER FOURTEEN

'ENOUGH of these mournful sighs,' Hester remonstrated impatiently. She slapped the latest report on Sasha's findings face-down on the table and eyed Sasha sternly. 'What's the problem?'

'I'm sorry...' Useless to deny her distraction of mind. She couldn't stop thinking that today was Monday, and in two days' time Nathan was to marry Urszula Budna.

Hester waved dismissively. 'Nothing to be sorry about. What's Nathan done?'

There was no evading the acute perception in Hester Wingate's piercing eyes. 'It's not his fault,' Sasha answered glumly.

'Of course it's his fault,' Hester corrected with asperity. 'Men are always at fault. Nathan is a man. *Ergo*, he is at fault.'

'There's this Polish woman...' Sasha started off circumspectly.

'There always is. Men have two brains. The one in the unmentionable area causes all the trouble.'

A burning rush of blood scorched Sasha's cheeks.

Hester put her own inimitable interpretation on that. 'Seduced you as well, did he? Swept you away with passion?'

'Not exactly. Only a little,' Sasha demurred, too honest to pretend she hadn't been a willing participant in their mutual desire.

'At least you're better than Elizabeth Maddox. That woman is mad. Megalomania.' Hester leaned over and patted Sasha's hand. 'Don't you worry. It will all turn out for the best.'

'It can't,' Sasha said hopelessly. 'He's contracted a marriage with someone else and he can't get out of it. He wrote the contract himself and it's watertight. You see . . .'

Sasha explained about Elizabeth's machinations to get both Nathan and Matt back to bolster her image for political purposes.

Hester rose from her chair. Her diminutive form shook with deep emotion. 'Blood will tell. He'll find a way. Rotten to the core like his great-grandfather, but essentially a good man. One of the finest. Blood will tell. He'll find a way.'

Hester could have been speaking Egyptian for all Sasha understood. 'Are you speaking of Nathan?'

'He even looks likes his great-grandfather. Got the devil in him. Always had. But I thought he had enough of *me* in him to correct for that.'

Nathan had never fitted into any family tree Hester had given her. There was one item Sasha could latch on to. 'Who was Nathan's great-grandfather?'

Hester looked sharply at her. 'Haven't you found that out yet?'

'No.' It wasn't in her brief from Hester.

'Not much good at digging up the dirt, are you?'

Sasha bridled at the premature criticism. 'That's not quite true,' she defended. 'I haven't found out all the ramifications yet, and I wasn't going to mention it until I'd worked my way through them, but...'

Sasha hesitated, mindful of the security that the nanny's quarters provided her and Bonnie. She was on dangerous ground with this, but her professional expertise had been called into question.

'Go on,' Hester urged.

'It's about Seagrave Dunworthy,' Sasha said slowly.

'Is it, now?' The interest kindled in Hester's eyes took a mega-leap at that name.

Sasha decided that her independent occupation of that part of the Mosman house no longer mattered. She burnt her bridges behind her. 'Seagrave Dunworthy attempted to enter a marriage that would have involved him in bigamy.'

Hester sat down, a look of triumph spreading across her face. 'Is that so?' she encouraged.

'Yes,' Sasha said firmly. 'I have proof of the existence of the first wife and she was alive at the time the second marriage was to take place.'

'Absolute proof?' Hester queried.

'Absolute,' Sasha assured her. 'Certificates double-checked. The second marriage was to take place at St. Mary's Cathedral, Bishop Clancy officiating. It was the social wedding of the year. The bride turned up. The groom turned up. So did the brother of the first wife, uninvited and unannounced.'

'I don't need the details of that part,' Hester said sharply.

'Of course, once the existence of the first wife was made known, the wedding could not go ahead.'

'Get on with the good dirt,' Hester encouraged. 'This part is boring.'

'The name of the bride was suppressed in the newspaper. It turned out she had lied about her age and didn't have parental consent. There were also implications that she was pregnant at the time.'

'I'm interested in Dunworthy,' Hester snapped. 'Not in some flighty female.'

'He died soon after. Within two years. The death certificate states the cause as a fall from a horse. Some say he invited death, others that it was by his own hand.'

'Nonsense!' Hester scoffed. 'He was simply careless.'

'A few close friends said it was from an excess of passion.'

'Aggravated remorse, more likely.'

'His first wife was institutionalised in Zurich for deep psychological problems.' The diagnosis on the medical report was schizophrenia, but Sasha knew that was the popular label for any mental disorder in those days.

'In a word, she was mad,' Hester declared.

'Yes. After her death . . .'

'When was that?'

'A month before he died.'

Hester frowned. 'You've got uncontestable proof of the date of her death?'

'Yes. And once he was free of his legal obligations to his first wife, Seagrave Dunworthy made his extraordinary will. It was signed one week before his fatal fall from a horse.'

Hester sat for a while in brooding silence. She finally gave Sasha a beetling look. 'He was a callous, unfeeling man.'

Sasha shrugged, not prepared to agree or disagree with that judgement.

'Is that all you've dug up on him?' Hester demanded.

'I haven't had time to work through all the trusts and find out what they mean. But I did find one thing. I think it's something important.'

She had Hester's keen attention.

'Among the papers I examined there were archival files from Brumby, Blackridge and Bagwell. They were Seagrave Dunworthy's solicitors. In the correspondence, reference was made to a Mary Ester Dawson...'

Sasha paused, looking for a reaction from Hester. It was one of the names in the Dawson family bible where the dates had been changed. Hester stared at her unblinkingly, giving nothing away, waiting for her to go on.

'The letter is dated a few days before he died. I think the letter was meant to be passed on, but no one realised its significance until it was too late. It wasn't passed on and he received no reply to it. After he died... well, there was no point to it any more. Until I found it.'

'You have it here?' Hester demanded gruffly.

'Yes.'

'What does it say?'

'It's too deeply personal for anyone but Mary Ester Dawson,' Sasha said quietly.

A flash of pain sharpened Hester's eyes. 'You know that's me.'

'I guessed.'

'Show it to me.'

Sasha lifted the photocopy out of her briefcase. The old lady's hand shook as she took the letter written over seventy years ago. She read it slowly, devouring every word, going back to the beginning, trying to comprehend.

Sasha felt intrusive. She got up and strolled along the veranda, pausing to look down at the lush tropical garden below. The frangipani trees were in full bloom. They were called love flowers, pink yellow, cream, so richly scented, growing everywhere. It made the place look exotic and warm and tended and cared for. Yet for over seventy years Hester Wingate had believed her life had been ruined by Seagrave Dunworthy. But for a careless oversight in a solicitor's office...

She heard Hester cough and turned around. There was a different look about her, a lifeless look. Her skin was like old parchment, her mouth withered, her eyes colourless.

'I misjudged him, didn't I?' she said bleakly.

'Yes.'

'Too late.'

'Not too late to tell the truth about him,' Sasha suggested, walking back to be with her.

A fleeting smile softened Hester's lips. 'He is Nathan's great-grandfather. He was my lover. He was the father of my child. And there was never another man to match him.'

'The items in the will, the rent for example...'

'It was to compel me to live in *his* house. It would never be economical to rent it out, and it couldn't be sold. It didn't work with me, of course. I've never put a foot inside that house. Ever.'

'Always to be spoken well of? Because of the gossip and calumnies and detractors?' Sasha prompted.

'He tried to make amends,' Hester acknowledged, 'but it was too late. I had him thrown out of the house. Took all his horses from him first, though. When I married George Wingate it wasn't much of a love match, but we did breed some of the finest thoroughbreds in the country.'

'It was Seagrave Dunworthy's love of horseflesh that made him put the rent in guineas.'

'We had so much in common. The day he died... that was the day I married George. When I heard about it, I told myself I was glad. Savagely glad. It made me free of him. But I wasn't free of him...'

'He loved you,' Sasha said gently. 'Deeply and passionately. He tried to do the honourable thing and marry you. There's a ring of desperation in that letter he sent to the solicitor. He might have been breaking the law, but it wasn't to hurt anyone. It was to set matters right. *When needs must...*'

A solitary tear formed in Hester's eye and it trickled a lonely path down her aged cheek. 'He never made me cry. Never.' Then, brokenly, '*When needs must...*'

Sasha curved her arm around Hester's frail shoulders. 'He loved you. There is no dirt.'

'I need to be alone. How is it that . . .'

'Yes?'

'. . . it took that old fool seventy years to make me cry?'

'I guess grief takes many forms,' Sasha said, aware that her bitter grief over the wasted years with Tyler had made her question the wisdom of her instinctive responses to Nathan. But not any more.

Life was too short to put off what she knew she wanted because of a set of irrevocable circumstances. Nathan might not fall off a horse tomorrow, but who was to say how long they would have together? It was stupid to brood over Nathan's paper marriage to a woman who had no rights to anything but a piece of paper in return. Sasha resolved not to let that stand in the way of what she and Nathan could have together.

She gave his great-grandmother an impulsive hug, then withdrew to pack away her papers and leave the old lady alone with her memories. She had walked to the end of the veranda when Hester called out. She paused and looked back. Hester was on her feet and hurrying after her.

'I didn't say thank you, Sasha.'

'It's just my job.'

'Thank you.'

Curiosity made Sasha ask, 'Would you mind telling me one last thing?'

'What is it?'

'The dates in the bible. I still don't know how and why they were altered. Was it because your younger brothers wanted to enlist in the army?'

'Good heavens, no! It was my sister, Isobel. I was with her while she did it.'

'So you could marry Seagrave?'

'My parents thought the age difference was too great.'

''But why did you pretend to me that you didn't know?'

'My dear, how else could I convince you I needed someone to work for me? If I hadn't found a job for you, Nathan would have made my life unbearable.' She gave Sasha a wise look. 'Take my word for it. When Nathan wants something he always finds a way.'

Sasha smiled. 'Thank you, Hester.'

On her way home, Sasha pondered the revelations that had answered so many questions in her mind. Nathan, being in the direct line of inheritance from Hester, would eventually become the owner of Seagrave Dunworthy's house. That was why he had the right to select who could rent rooms. That was why Elizabeth had considered she had a chance of inheriting, if Nathan had married her again.

What she found inconsistent with everything else Nathan had done was leaving it to chance whether she would come to his house and take up the offer of rooms. If she hadn't done that, and she might not have, they would have missed each other, because he had no way of finding her again. Yet, once she had come, he had gone out of his way to get her a job, as though it was important to him to keep her with him, even though he had already contracted a marriage with Urszula Budna. Somehow it didn't quite gell to Sasha.

Not that it mattered now. The past was the past. Holding faith with the future she and Nathan would share together was the important thing. When she arrived home and collected Bonnie from Marion's care, she told Marion that Matt was welcome to come up to the nursery after he got home from his playschool. She could not let the little boy feel unwanted any longer.

An hour later, Matt came pelting up the back stairs. He burst into the nursery, his face alight with pride and pleasure as he held up a big sheet of paper for Sasha and Bonnie to see.

'We did finger-painting today. This is my picture.'

Sasha regarded the stick figures with the expected interest. 'I like the colours you used, Matt.'

'Yes. I did you in pink, Bonnie.'

She obligingly gurgled her approval from the playpen.

'This is Daddy in blue,' Matt went on. 'Harry's in green for the garden. I made Marion orange 'cause she gives me orange juice every morning. I'm brown. That's getting dirty from playing.'

He seemed reluctant to identify the last stick person. 'And the one in red?' Sasha prompted.

Matt gave her a shy but hopeful look. 'That's my pretend mother.'

'Well, she looks very nice and warm,' Sasha said with a smile. 'Would you like me to pin the picture up on the wall? Then we can look at it whenever we want to.'

Matt eagerly agreed and Sasha invited him to choose the best position for it. He watched her press the thumbtacks in. Then they both stood back to admire the result.

'The teacher said to paint our family,' Matt informed her.

'You did a fine job, Matt.'

It was Nathan's voice behind them.

'Daddy!' Matt ran to his father and Nathan swung him up for a hug. 'I can play up here now, Daddy.'

Nathan's eyes met Sasha's with an oddly tense and urgent look. 'Well, how about you play with Bonnie while I talk to her mummy, Matt?' he said, his voice warmly encouraging for his son.

There was instant agreement. With both children in the playpen, happily gathering and scattering plastic blocks, Nathan quickly drew Sasha into the adjoining kitchenette. He slid his hands around her waist, drawing her close, but his mind was not on kissing her. His eyes searched hers with an intensity that set her heart aflutter.

'There may be a way out of the contract. It's extreme. It's radical. And it involves you, Sasha.'

CHAPTER FIFTEEN

HESTER was right, Sasha thought, her mind leaping with elation. When Nathan really wanted something, he found a way. Matt was right. His daddy *could* do anything.

Sasha flung her arms around his neck, her eyes sparkling with a great burst of happiness. 'You're the most wonderful man I've ever met!' As well as the sexiest. She went up on her toes to kiss him.

Nathan hesitated a moment, a brief conflict in his eyes. Desire won. His mouth took hers with passionate intensity. His arms pulled her into a fiercely possessive embrace. Arousal was so swift, Sasha broke away in alarm as she remembered the children.

'Matt and Bonnie...'

'I love you, Sasha.'

Her heart swelled anew. 'I love you, too.'

He looked deeply and seriously into her eyes. 'I need your help.'

'What do you want me to do?'

'Give me Tyler's address.'

Sasha was thunderstruck. 'What's Tyler got to do with you and me and Urszula Budna?'

'He's the linchpin to my present difficulties. Anyone who can bed Elizabeth and not feel unmanned has

extraordinary powers, including tenacity of purpose.
Tyler is the man I need for a desperate task. In mili-
tary terms he'd be called "the forlorn hope". Not
much chance of survival.'

'Radical' and 'extreme' suddenly took on a terrible
meaning. Sasha shook her head vehemently. 'Not
murder, Nathan. I've thought of that, too, but only
figuratively, not literally. No, no, no, no, no! Not
murder. And I don't believe Tyler would be capable of
it anyway. He's irresponsible, occasionally violent, but
definitely not a murderer.'

Nathan looked at her in amazement. 'You actually
thought of murdering Urszula Budna?'

'Not really. It flashed through my mind. But I only
wanted her to go away.' She felt defensive.

'You thought I'd contemplate murder?' There was
a certain amount of awe in his voice.

'Not until this moment, no.'

'Perish the thought. You're never to think such a
thing again.'

'I won't.' She hadn't really thought of it at all.
She thought Nathan had. To distract his attention, she
swivelled around to get a notebook and pen from the
top kitchen drawer. 'I'll write down Tyler's address for
you.'

Having done that, she tore off the page and handed
it to Nathan, who quickly pocketed it then produced
some papers of his own.

'I need you to sign these,' he said, spreading them
on the kitchen bench.

'What are they?'

'Sasha...' He grasped her arms and turned her around to him. His riveting blue eyes bored into her heart again. 'Will you marry me?'

She took a deep breath to clear the sudden obstruction in her throat. 'I'd consider it if you weren't married to someone else.'

'I love you.'

'I won't commit bigamy.'

'I love you passionately.'

'We don't *need* to marry. But if there's a way...'

'There's a way.'

'I don't want you to mess up my life.'

'Mine's already messed up.'

'That's your fault.'

'Kiss me.'

'The children...'

'...won't see a thing.' He eased her back against the kitchen sink.

'You know what this leads to,' Sasha protested, aware of the thrill of excitement already quivering down her thighs.

'Only a kiss.'

'One.'

'As long as it lasts to the end of time.'

'No.'

'If you sign the papers I'll go and see Tyler.'

She grabbed up the pen again. 'This is only to get rid of you.'

'Here's the line.'

'This is an application to marry under special licence!'

'Covering all eventualities.'

She eyed him in alarm. *When needs must...* the words echoed through her mind. Was he the reincarnation of his great-grandfather? 'I haven't said yes yet.'

'This is not a contract. It's an application that can always be nullified.'

'Are you sure?'

'Certain.'

'I'll write that on it. This application can be nullified at any time.'

'Fine. It's always best to be cautious.'

Sasha was. Particularly over this point. Nathan had a definite tendency to take the law into his own hands.

'Thank you, my love.' He whipped the papers away the moment she'd finished writing, stole a quick kiss on her lips, then was off. 'I'll be back as soon as I've got Tyler lined up.'

'For what?' Sasha called after him.

'Best you don't know.'

He was gone.

Sasha couldn't follow him. The children needed her supervision. So she stewed over the plan, whatever it might be, for a considerable amount of time. Then she gave up on it. Nathan Parnell was a law unto himself. She might as well get used to living dangerously. He had certainly spoiled her for any other man.

Afternoon passed into evening. Dinner was eaten. The children were put to bed. Sasha went to bed herself after hours of impatience, waiting for Nathan to return.

She was woken by a nibble on her ear. 'Sasha, we're going to marry.' The words whispered through her mind. For a moment she wondered if she was dreaming. Then an arm curled around her waist and she rolled onto her back to check out the reality of the man lying in the bed beside her. Her lover. Her husband-to-be if he spoke the truth.

'I haven't set the date for a wedding,' she said, feeling she should be annoyed with Nathan for keeping her in the dark.

'I have.' He dropped a kiss on her nose.

Sasha sighed. What was the point in being petty? She loved him. She wanted him. And he was offering her the ultimate commitment to their relationship. 'What's your plan, Nathan?' she asked.

His lips grazed seductively over hers. 'It's a tight schedule.'

'How tight?'

'We get married an hour before I'm due to marry Urszula Budna.'

Sasha jack-knifed in shock, their heads bumping painfully as she knocked Nathan aside. She was too agitated to care. 'You're going to commit bigamy with her?' she squawked.

'No.' He pressed her down onto the pillow again and stroked her hair soothingly. 'If I'm already married to you, obviously I can't specifically perform the terms of the contract with her. It'd be against the law. A married man can't marry someone else.'

'That's true,' Sasha agreed on a wave of deep relief. 'But Urszula isn't going to be happy. And she's got Elizabeth as her lawyer.'

'That's where Tyler comes in.'

'How?'

'Firstly, he and Joshua McDougal will be witnesses at our wedding. Apart from showing Urszula our certificate of marriage, they can also swear to her that the deed has been done.'

Incredulity flooded Sasha's mind. 'You got Tyler to agree to that?'

'Yes. Then he'll marry Urszula in my place, giving her the right to stay in Australia and take out citizenship. Which was all she wanted from our contract before she got other ideas.'

'Tyler? Marry Urszula?' Sasha knew for a fact Tyler didn't believe in marriage.

'He doesn't have to live with her. He doesn't have to stay married to her. It's only a convenient legality,' Nathan explained patiently. 'He understands that.'

'How on earth did you persuade him into it?'

'I promised to save him from going to gaol. He needs legal representation for what he did to Elizabeth's car. I'm going to defend him. No one else could bring the same feelings of sympathy, understanding and compassion to the case that I will. Already I'm working on my peroration to the jury. I'll get him off.'

Sasha stared at him in dazed bewilderment. 'But that case won't come up before Wednesday. And Tyler thinks marriage is a gaol.'

'Not this one. No responsibility involved. It could be a perfect match. A marriage made in heaven. And it's another poke in the eye for Elizabeth. Tyler rather relishes that.'

'Ego. One-upmanship,' Sasha murmured. It fitted Tyler's character.

'Apart from which, what I'm going to pay him for marrying Urszula...' Nathan grinned. 'In Tyler's terms, it's the equivalent of winning Lotto.'

'A million dollars!'

'Nothing like it. But enough for Tyler to think he's got lucky for the first time in his life.'

Nathan started kissing her. His hands moved to do distracting things to her body. Sasha wanted to respond, but there was a clamour in her mind that insisted he was making a bigger mess out of the mess they already had. She lifted his head up, gulped in a quick breath and spilled out the worrying concerns he had raised.

'Can you afford it, Nathan?'

'For you, yes.'

'After we've paid for all this, are we going to be impoverished for the rest of our lives?'

Nathan told her what he was worth.

'Good heavens!' she gasped. 'Money like that can cause a lot of problems.'

'Sasha, darling, can we please face that problem when we come to it? The first thing is to get married. Let's concentrate only on that.'

She gradually relaxed. It was really rather marvellous thinking of how very much Nathan wanted them to be together and stay together. It added a special glow to their lovemaking, a deeper appreciation of his love and need for her. She smiled to herself as she remembered Nathan scorning love, saying it caused havoc and created chaos. He certainly thought it worth having now. Not pie-in-the-sky at all.

It was the real deep-down love this time. Sasha
could feel it in her soul. Perhaps the passion would not
stay as white-hot as it was now, but it was not a madness that would cool after eighteen months. It was
bonded in with mutual values, mutual beliefs, mutual
feelings, mutual instincts. Sasha knew the caring and
sharing and the continual building of both would always be ongoing for her and Nathan, the ready support of each other, the wanting that couldn't even
begin to envisage wanting anyone else.

He was her man.

She was his woman.

As they lay languorously together, feeling the sweet
bliss of utter contentment in the fulfilment of every
desire, Sasha's thoughts drifted over all Nathan's radical arrangements. She hoped nothing would go wrong
between now and Wednesday.

'Where are we being married?' she asked.

'Central Register Office. It's near St Mary's Cathedral.'

Sasha thought of Hester and her aborted marriage
to Seagrave Dunworthy. A church wedding didn't
guarantee anything. Neither did all the flowers and
finery that went with it. That wasn't the important
part at all. Not to Sasha. The Central Register Office
was fine by her.

'I must tell my parents,' she said, more as a reminder to herself than as a remark to Nathan.

'No!' he yelled like a scalded cat. The next instant
he had her flat on her back and was leaning over her
in urgent command. 'You mustn't tell anyone. Not a
soul. Not even Marion. It was bad enough that I had

to go to your parents concerning the details of the
marriage application.'

'How did you know where they live?'

'Umm ... I suppose I looked it up in the telephone
directory.'

Sasha knew that was wrong. Her parents had an
unlisted number. She wondered what Nathan was being evasive about, then shrugged off the thought. It
was irrelevant.

'Why mustn't anyone be told? Surely family can
know. It's not as if...'

'Sasha, people talk. Can't help themselves. Then
other people talk to other people, and word gets
around. Imagine this scenario. You're standing there
as the bride. I'm standing beside you as the groom.
And the question is posed ... is there any impediment
to stop this man and woman from marrying?'

Her mind instantly flew to Hester and Seagrave.

'The last thing we need,' Nathan said vehemently,
'is Urszula Budna's brother turning up and waving a
legal contract that I'm in breach of. Can you even begin to comprehend what a disaster that would be, and
how the past repeats itself?'

CHAPTER SIXTEEN

THE past did not repeat itself.

At ten o'clock on Wednesday morning, Sasha and Nathan were married in the Central Register Office. It did not have the grandeur of St Mary's Cathedral. A bishop did not officiate. But no one turned up to stop the marriage.

Owing to the secrecy that was maintained, Sasha was unable to wear a wedding-dress. However, she had spent part of Tuesday doing Christmas shopping. The present she bought for herself was a very expensive white silk suit. Sasha found it very easy to convince herself that her wedding-day was better than any Christmas Day she could ever have. It was perfectly reasonable, therefore, to open and wear her Christmas gift to herself on this more appropriate occasion.

Nathan, of course, looked as handsome as ever. In keeping with decorum, he wore a conservative but very smart grey suit.

The ceremony was brief. Efficient but effective, Sasha thought. Nevertheless, it had an unexpected and dazzling highlight. Nathan not only slid a wedding-ring on to the third finger of her left hand. He accompanied it with another ring featuring a fabulous pink Argyle diamond. It choked Sasha up for several moments. She looked at Nathan with swimming eyes. He assisted her in regaining her composure by kissing her until a surge of heat dried the tears.

Tyler and Joshua performed their role as witnesses with perfect aplomb, making it look as though it was an everyday event in their lives. They expressed congratulations, shook Nathan's hand warmly, kissed Sasha on both cheeks, and generally conducted themselves as though they were thoroughly delighted with the successful completion of phase one of *the plan*. They strolled outside to await the arrival of the next bride. At precisely eleven o'clock, a white Mercedes with government plates on it pulled up at the curb.

Out stepped a man who frowned at Sasha.

'The brother,' Nathan murmured.

He was followed by a woman who was quite strikingly beautiful and voluptuously curved.

'Urszula,' Nathan murmured.

Sasha reflected that she could have felt savagely jealous if Nathan's rings weren't on her finger.

There was a sharp intake of breath from Tyler.

Sasha cynically suspected he wouldn't mind consummating his paper marriage.

Then out of the car stepped Elizabeth Maddox.

'The lawyer,' Nathan murmured.

Elizabeth drew herself up to her full height for the purpose of looking down her nose at the waiting group.

'Your choice of witnesses, Nathan,' she invited, as if preparing for a duel with pistols. She ignored Sasha.

With a wave of his hand Nathan indicated Tyler and Joshua.

'What poor taste you have!' Elizabeth observed coldly.

'I think introductions are in order,' Nathan replied. 'This is my wife, Sasha Parnell. Beside me is my replacement bridegroom for Urszula. You have met before. His name is Tyler Cullum.'

Hell broke loose.

Elizabeth's strident responses indicated that not only were the dogs of war unleashed, but also the four horsemen of the Apocalypse. What was being called down upon their heads was about to make Armageddon look like a children's play yard.

Urszula's brother broke into violent argument and agitation. He saw a life of ease and luxury evaporating before his eyes.

Elizabeth went into legal argument as to why the marriage was void. Nathan urged Sasha to come home and consummate immediately. Elizabeth's blood-pressure soared to a new medical record before she conceded bitter defeat to a *fait accompli,* and turned her attention to punitive damages.

Urszula gave emotional outcries of piteous horror at the situation.

At this critical moment, Tyler stepped forward and into the ring. Urszula surreptitiously cast a glance over him as she held a hand to her bleeding heart.

'Pain and agony!' Elizabeth ranted in triumph. 'You'll pay for pain and agony. You'll pay for loss of reputation to my client. You'll pay for abrogation of her rights, arrogation of powers you don't possess, and derogation to Tyler Cullum...'

Tyler smiled at Urszula. It was a full blast double whammy smile of explosive impact. Many a lady had felt the full blast of Tyler's smile. Few recovered.

Urszula was no exception. The legal argument going on around her was falling on barren ground. Urszula was a realist. She half smiled back at Tyler.

Tyler had many attractions. At his charming best, most women would look and keep looking. Urszula kept looking. Sasha observed a certain animal magnetism flowing between Tyler and Urszula. Sasha understood that. She wondered if Urszula would like a trip to the great interior of Australia.

Tyler seized the moment.

He stepped forward and took Urszula's hands in his. 'You're the woman I've been waiting for all my life,' he said with winning fervour. 'I can make you happier than you've ever been before. I've got the money and I've got the time. I'll take photos of you that will be featured in every magazine in the country. You'll be famous.'

'I will?' Urszula's eyes filled with stars. 'Yes,' she said. 'Yes, I'd like that.'

'Don't listen to him,' Elizabeth snapped.

'I'll give you everything,' Tyler promised. 'Everything a woman can want. In return I require one thing.'

'Not children. I don't want children,' Urszula said anxiously.

'I have all I need,' Tyler assured her hastily.

'Then what do you want?'

'Fire your lawyer.'

Urszula turned a glazed look to Elizabeth. 'You're fired.'

Tyler curled Urszula's arm around his and swept his bride-to-be into the register office. Joshua belatedly followed, looking perfectly relaxed about all that had transpired.

'No, Urszula, no!' her brother yelled, running after her.

'Go and marry Elizabeth,' Urszula hurled back at him. 'I've got what I want.'

Elizabeth screamed a tirade of abuse after Tyler's retreating back. What she would do to him in court would be nothing compared to what she would do if she ever had him at her mercy.

'Time for us to leave,' Nathan said to Sasha. 'Now we can start planning a proper wedding and a proper honeymoon and a proper everything.'

'Don't they need a second witness in there?' Sasha didn't want any hitches in phase two of *the plan*.

'Let the brother come to his senses. I'm sure he will. Otherwise they'll have to use a clerk.'

The door of Elizabeth's Mercedes slammed shut. The car surged forward, away from the kerb, and Nathan stood looking after it for quite some moments.

'What are you thinking, darling?' Sasha asked, drawing his attention back to her.

'Elizabeth is a most erratic driver,' he said cheerfully, taking her hand. 'Let's go home. For ourselves. And for the children.'

WHEN NATHAN explained what their marriage meant to his son, Matt's eyes glowed with satisfaction in his own inner belief. 'I knew she was my mother. She's not my pretend mother any more. She's real.'

Nathan clearly had no inclination to correct him, yet fact was fact, and he could hardly ignore Elizabeth's natural claim on their son. Matt did have to understand in case Elizabeth still persisted in wanting custody.

'Matt, the other lady who came last week . . .'

'You were wrong about her, Daddy,' the little boy said with unshakeable conviction.

'Why am I wrong, Matt?'

''Cause it wasn't in her eyes.'

From the mouths of babes came the simplest of truths, Sasha thought. Elizabeth was his biological mother, but that had no meaning whatsoever to Matt. Maybe he was right.

He turned to Sasha, his eyes clear with the knowledge that was so clear to him. 'I felt it inside when you looked at me. Like at the park when you said you were sorry you had to go. And at playschool when I told the other kids.'

Her empathy for his loneliness.

'I felt it too, Matt,' she said softly. She crouched down to draw him closer to her, their eyes sharing the same knowledge. 'What your daddy was trying to tell you . . . the other lady is your birth mother. But I'm your real mother in here.' She pressed one hand to her heart and the other over Matt's heart. 'I always will be.'

They shared a secret smile of perfect understanding.

Then Matt turned his smile up to his father, 'See, Daddy?'

'Yes, I see, Matt.' The look he turned to Sasha was all she wanted to see. The deep forever love that would see them through their lives.

SASHA TOLD Nathan the proper wedding and proper honeymoon could wait until some time in the New Year. What she wanted most of all was a family Christmas.

The next day a huge van arrived in the driveway. It took four men to carry a large fir tree in a huge pot into the lounge. Only a room with a fourteen-foot ceiling could have accommodated such a tree.

They spent hours decorating it. When the happy task was finally completed, and Nathan switched on the string of coloured lights he'd draped around the branches, Bonnie thought it so wonderful, she took her first tottering steps.

On Christmas Day, Sasha's parents came to share in the festivities. The roast turkey had just been set on the dining-table when the doorbell rang. Sasha and Marion had their hands full bringing in all the accompanying dishes to serve with the turkey, so Nathan went to answer the call.

There was a murmur of voices. Sasha idly wondered who it could be. She didn't have to wait long to find out. Brooks entered the room, his arms laden with presents. Jane followed, carrying a big plate containing a massive plum pudding surrounded by bon-bons for the children. Behind them came a voice that Sasha recognised all too well.

Hester Wingate.

She entered the room, complaining bitterly as Nathan ushered her in before him. 'I broke my word. I swore I'd never enter this house that Seagrave built for me.' She found Sasha's eye and looked sternly at her. 'But I can hardly go to meet him on the other side without knowing he had done a proper job of it, can I?'

Sasha hastened to her side, uttering reassurances. 'Of course, you had to come and see for yourself. We'll set three more places at the table for you and Jane and Brooks, and have Christmas dinner together. Afterwards I'll show you through all the rooms.'

'I'd like that,' Hester agreed, 'but I still think I did better taking all his horses.'

'I'm sure that's right,' Sasha said, inwardly rejoicing that Hester had finally found peace and goodwill to all men. Especially with Seagrave Dunworthy.

LATER THAT NIGHT, when their visitors went home and the children were tucked up in bed asleep, Sasha and Nathan relaxed together on one of the chesterfields in the lounge. The lights were out except for those on the tree, and they reminisced over the day in a mood of blissful contentment.

'Life is full of chance,' Sasha mused. 'If we hadn't met in the park, if Tyler hadn't turned up, if I hadn't been desperate for a place to live, you would never have found me, Nathan.'

'Sasha, my darling, after we met in the park, nothing was left to chance. It was only a matter of time.'

'How could you be so sure I would come here?'

'I wasn't.'

'What would have happened if I hadn't turned up?'

'I would have come to you.'

She turned on him in exasperation. 'You didn't know where I lived. Or where I might have moved to.'

He grinned. 'Yes, I did.'

She suddenly recollected that he had found her parents' address, and not through the telephone directory. 'How?' she demanded.

His grin grew wider. 'Computer games.'

She heaved an impatient sigh. 'Stop teasing.'

'When I slipped the address of this house into your bag, I also slipped in a tiny technological device.'

'You bugged me?'

'No, darling. That's against the law,' he said sanctimoniously. 'I was simply tracking your bag. Wherever it went.'

'What if I'd left it in a bus? Or had it stolen?'

'The first stop gave me your parents' address. I figured they'd always know where you were.'

'Promise that you'll never do such a thing again.'

'I promise.'

'Why did you do it?'

'Because, my love, I was in need of a wife.'

Hi!

*The last thing I
expected—or needed—
when I arrived in
Copenhagen was a
lecture. But that's
what Rune Christensen
proceeded to give me.
He clearly blames me
for the disappearance
of my sister and his
nephew. If only Rune
wasn't so attractive.*

Love, Gina

MILLION DOLLAR SWEEPSTAKES (III)

THE VENGEFUL GROOM
Sara Wood

Legend has it that those married in Eternity's chapel are destined for a lifetime of happiness. But happiness isn't what Giovanni wants from marriage—it's revenge!

Ten years ago, Tina's testimony sent Gio to prison—for a crime he didn't commit. *Now* he's back in Eternity and looking for a bride. *Now* Tina is about to learn just how ruthless and disturbingly sensual Gio's brand of vengeance can be.

THE VENGEFUL GROOM, available in October from Harlequin Presents, is the fifth book in Harlequin's new cross-line series, **WEDDINGS, INC.** Be sure to look for the sixth book, **EDGE OF ETERNITY,** by Jasmine Cresswell (Harlequin Intrigue #298), coming in November.

WED5

HARLEQUIN®

PRESENTS *plus*

One brief encounter had disastrously altered their futures, leaving Antonia with deep psychological scars and Patrick accused of a horrific crime. Will the passion that exists between them be enough to heal their wounds?

Fler knows she's in for some serious heartache when she falls for Kyle Ranburn, the man who caused her daughter so much pain. But she has no idea how difficult it is to be torn by her love for the two of them.

Fall in love with Patrick and Kyle—Antonia and Fler do!

Watch for

Wounds of Passion by Charlotte Lamb
Harlequin Presents Plus #1687

and

Dark Mirror by Daphne Clair
Harlequin Presents Plus #1688

Harlequin Presents Plus
The best has just gotten better!

Available in October wherever Harlequin books are sold.

This September, discover the fun of falling in love with...

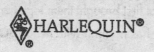

Harlequin is pleased to bring you this exciting new collection of three original short stories by bestselling authors!

ELISE TITLE
BARBARA BRETTON
LASS SMALL

LOVE AND LAUGHTER—sexy, romantic, fun stories guaranteed to tickle your funny bone and fuel your fantasies!

Available in September wherever
Harlequin books are sold.

HARLEQUIN®

MIRA™

The brightest star in women's fiction!

This October, reach for the stars and watch all your
dreams come true with **MIRA BOOKS.**

HEATHER GRAHAM POZZESSERE
Slow Burn in October
An enthralling tale of murder and passion set against
the dark and glittering world of Miami.

SANDRA BROWN
The Devil's Own in November
She made a deal with the devil…but she didn't bargain
on losing her heart.

BARBARA BRETTON
Tomorrow & Always in November
Unlikely lovers from very different worlds… They had to
cross time to find one another.

PENNY JORDAN
For Better For Worse in December
Three couples, three dreams—can they rekindle the love
and passion that first brought them together?

The sky has no limit with **MIRA BOOKS.**